NEW NEW ANIMALS

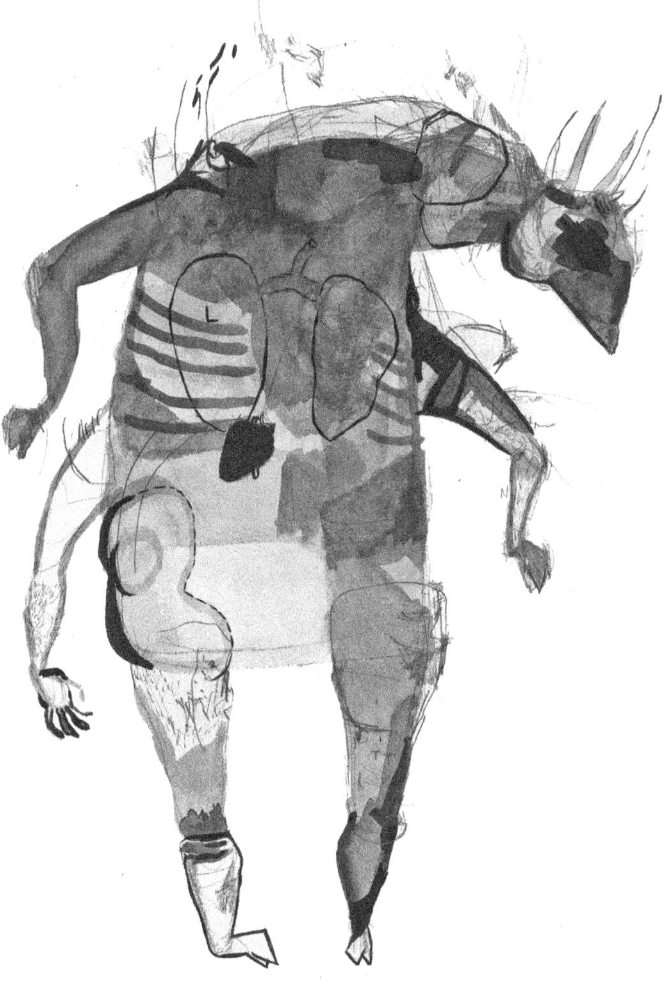

NICK FRANCIS POTTER

New New Animals
by Nick Francis Potter

ISBN 978-1-940853-24-6

Published by Calamari Archive, Ink.
https://www.calamaripress.com

CONTENTS

NEW NEW ANIMALS

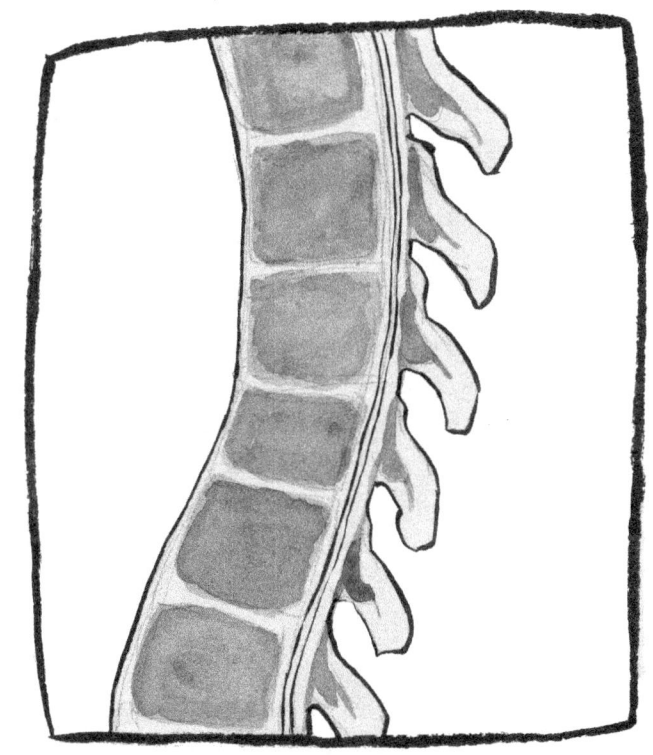

THE WREATH OPTION

I'm in about middle school when Father starts developing a language in the attic that can carve the marrow from your bones. I first hear the filth through the ceiling one day after school. Mother is sitting at the kitchen table, her hands folded below it, sort of listening, I guess, and practicing stillness.

"What's Father doing up there?" I ask her.

"Fine-tuning his new words on the cats," she says.

"Mother, does he like me?"

"Oh heavens, boy, I don't think so," she says and shakes her face at her lap like she means to say she's pretty sure.

It is about this same time I start to take notice of the itch in my skeleton parts. Day after day, that sooty language is falling through the ceiling and leaving sharpish bits of consonants all on the counter tops, all *psts* and *cfks* and *shts*. What's more, I think the words leaked through the attic floor carve mother most. You figure it by the contraptions she uses. It takes all sorts of ropes and pulleys and things to stand her up now, when it used to take just a stick.

I tell all this to Richard.

Richard has been advising me about Father for a week or so now, mostly just listening. When I tell him about Father, he doesn't look at me but points his ear at me and starts a cassette to roll it all up. He puts notes in his pad too. He wants a good history so we can suss the best option for removal. Richard's taller than Father, with a slight slant in his spine that sends his chin forward over his shoes and a short bristle of hair on his lip. He's been helpful all the way through, talking removal the whole time. I find myself wondering if Richard has kids.

• • •

This is a thing to know about my father: one day when I am not much of a ten-year-old at all and Father still does father things outdoors, I find a map in his closet. This is back when pretending still works, gets me into places that I've not been back to since. I find the map easy because it has my name on it in big blue letters up at the top, in there in the closet on the floor. It looks like he worked it up while I was still in Mother's belly, back when Mother says that Father used to wear ties and pants. On the map, he's got me planned out as a top-grade bird trainer, fluent in the squawking and everything, just like him. There are upward lines with arrows and notches and things all about it. It's like a son map, I guess.

And I guess I take a long time looking at it because he finds me and decides to quick father me, like right then and there. He looks at me and something like *what the hell* is in his eyes for a few seconds and then he smacks my face crooked. Naturally, I'm not much interested in this kind of fathering, so I dive back behind Mother's dresses, but he's fathering so fast now, he grabs me, catches me by my ankle and drags me down the stairs into the kitchen. There he props me up stiff in a chair, sloshes my head with sugar soda, the orange kind, and starts cutting out pieces of my hair with a butter knife. The cutting is sticky and irritating like everything, but still I say, "Thank you, sir," just trying to son this fathering properly, encouragingly, as a courtesy, really.

Richard says that courtesy is important, but he feels that fathers can take advantage of it at times. He tells me that was what courtesy was like back then, okay, but courtesy these days is we respect our fathers by stopping our fathers from fathering themselves deep into the ground. I tend to agree with him. He tells it nice, Richard.

• • •

Father doesn't much care for me after I find the map, and I can see why, my being a straight turkey up in his closet and all. Truth be told, I don't really remember a thing before the map and my orange sugar soda haircut, or if I do, it isn't anything better. Father grew me up on sticks, rocks, and words, all of them.

It's a task trying to think up any times without his shadow there even. My pretendings have gone muted, dusty in the crooks. I can't wiggle a finger or he knows, and I just can't seem to get to pretending without a movement of some kind. It's a bit easier at night, but not much, they tuck me in so tight. The old toys and TV games have since been charred as well. There are still tiny trains in the basement and a track, but I haven't been let to touch them ever since I've been able to closet a thought. Father and Mother never have at them either, so they're left to chug at me quietly whenever I pass the basement door.

• • •

Richard asks me questions sometimes, about Father's methods and things, if I've uncovered any reasons behind them or anything like that.

It's just his way, I tell him. He does fathering that really gets stuck in your ears, gloms onto your skin. I'm not much for it myself, but it's his way, and I'm his son.

Have you ever wondered why fathers feel it's necessary to hollow out your bones so good? As a child I wasn't allowed to think about it much, but I have had plans to think about it for a while. And now that I can, it's hard to know where to start my thoughts at. I can't think my way into the attic really because I haven't been there since even before middle school, so usually I start at the front door and manage my way into my bedroom. It's worth trying, exercising anything left between the ears.

Richard doesn't seem to know the answers all the time. He is working on papers to figure it out, has been for quite a while. He says he was up transcribing late last night, punching up a bid for approval from the county. These things get messy, he says.

• • •

Another thing to know: I am in high school, and Father is yelling at Mother and me in his perfect bone hollowing tongue, *psts* and *cfks* and *shts* slurring and spattering and sharper than ever, and I feel my ribs starting to bow at the sounds, and just as I am wondering how much more I can stomach, Mother shouts, "That's it!" and then, "I'm finished!" and she just walks right out of there, right out the front door, and he stops speaking, straight right then. And she's never come back. And he hasn't spoken since.

What he does instead is start drinking things, not that he didn't drink things before, but now he's drinking special things in order to ferment his breath. I suspect it's a way for him to announce his presence in silence, to put across his distaste for me, which was always one of his foremost talking points during his language days. He soaks his mouth studiously for months with a concoction of rare liquors, river water, and coiled ropes of black licorice. Now, even in silence, he radiates anger and hate. He's even trained himself to breathe only through his mouth, his jaw hanging loose and wide, to promote the rank effect.

One day I stumble into the kitchen and there he is, reading the paper in his fatherly manner, tieless, pantless, his mouth agape. I take up a bowl for cereal and he, still eyeing the paper, turns his head toward me and exhales hotly. I pass out, only to wake up hours later, when everything is dark and Father is stretched out and asleep in the bed where he and Mother used to sleep, only now it's just him there. It's kept me in my walking strategies, struggling to stay out of reach of his breath ever since. I ask Richard why fathers tend toward such wretchedness. I mean, you'd never expect it from such a short, sinewy man as Father is now. These late days and him always holding fists aloft and walking his criminal walk. It's like he's lost his fear someplace and no one's helped him to find it.

Richard says we can change that.

• • •

Richard tells me I'm man-sized now, the inheritor of these bricks and wood, this rectangle of shallow grass. I figure I can more than help Father find the thing he's lost. It's why I'm visiting an advisor in the first place, one who deals with adult children and their animal fathers.

Today, Richard says the paperwork went through, so we can finally review my options. He hands me some pamphlets and a breakdown of package plans. He even puts my name on a map and everything to chart the event. In light of it all, the haircuts and marrow loss, Mother and the map and the birds and the *psts* and *cfks* and *shts,* Richard suggests the Wreath Option.

"You know," he says, "the Wreath Option is pretty popular."

"The Wreath Option?"

"The Wreath Option," he says again, hands me a purple pamphlet.

"Is this what you'd pick?"

"Well, based on what you've told me. Considering your position in the home, the property and all."

He later discloses to me what he chose for his father. He says he picked the River Option, shows me the blue pamphlet. I don't know why he tells me and am pretty sure it's against their company policy. I suspect it makes us some kind of friends for him to do it.

I look close at the Wreath Option for a while. There is a list of necessaries I need to have before the thing can happen:

- 5mm X 50' rope of veritable strength (3)
- 12" bricklayer's hammer
- 2 gallons of dirt water
- 10' X 24" roll of galvanized chicken wire
- medical gloves (3 pairs, for layering)
- 12' X 16' polyethylene tarp
- industrial strength shears

After we review the details one more time, I feel confident in my decision. Richard doesn't know it, but before I leave I overheard him and his manager low-talking about my prospects for success. It doesn't bother me much. Things are clear. This is the way to son a father with proper courtesy and honor, the right way for me and for him.

· · ·

Following the instructions, the whole thing goes really quick and simple. I come up from behind and grip around Father's forehead with one hand, place the other hand beneath his chin. I do this twist move they teach you in the pamphlet, but I do it wrong I guess, because instead of what he's supposed to do, he turns around to face me. His jaw is broken now and his mouth is dropped open and the stench is unbearable and he's looking at me again like what the hell, but he's still silent as ever, so I step behind him and try my twist move again and this time he falls quick, just like the pamphlet said.

Richard said that after the initial twist, things usually run pretty smoothly, and he's right: propping him up on his knees, I lay Father's head back like it's on a kind of head-hinge and reach in to extract the spine, which turns out to be kind of like threading a really big screw, taking a while, and I can totally understand the purpose of the three pairs of gloves at this point, but then eventually that's over too.

I curl the vertebrae into a circle, contain it in chicken wire, and hang it on the front door. Richard said he'd come by to help with the cleanup, but really the tarp has managed to contain most of it, and so here I am, all done, a most courteous and proper son, now with a brand new wreath.

TEMPORARY GOLIATH

TEMPORARILY

1

Jilly Zimsky, slack-armed pioneer, hand-pulling potential: a wagon full of fist-sized rocks. Down in the gully dicking around, chucking rocks, establishing an imagination. Easy peasy.

2

Discover:

Walk far enough, into Calloway's oilfield, meet Marlow, temporary Goliath.

Hello, little missus—no farther please. We've an oilfield out here, you'll notice, Marlow identifying the individual oil wells with his index finger: *there, there, and there...* [swinging his arm] *and over there.*

Wait a second now, you're a Zimsky girl, aren't you.

Nodding.

I thought so. I used to date your mom in high school.

3

Kill Marlow.

4

Jilly Zimsky pulls a smaller rock from her wagon, placing it in her mouth, her cheeks wide-freckling in the oilfield air. It's hot enough out it melts her pioneering mascara. Warpaint, somewhat: oil derricks operating softly in the distance. A light wind gets into her face and Jilly, tickled, brushes her nose with the heel of her hand.

Unwomanly. Pioneerish.

She pulls the rock out from her mouth with her slender fingers. She uses the breadth of her imagination, recently broadened, to start a conversation.

5

Marlow saying, *Oh, well, I'm the, uh, oilfield Goliath here. Who else?*

Jilly Zimsky saying, *You're a lot smaller than someone expects. You say you're a Goliath?*

Marlow saying, *Temporarily. Keepin' people out of the oilfields, you know. That kind of stuff...*

Marlow saying, *What about you, then? What is it you do?*

Jilly Zimsky: *I'm a pioneer. I do pioneering, invent animals, destroy histories—you can figure it out...I keep myself supplied with a wagon of rocks.*

Gesturing to the rocks.

Marlow saying, *Oh. I see.*

6

What's that?

Marlow and Marlow's folding chair, folding table, and a stack of paper for folding (ways to occupy time). And on the ground: what she's looking at at his feet: a city in miniature, built out of copier paper and spreading across the perimeter of Calloway's oilfield—a small-scale reproduction of Jilly's hometown—and Jilly,

It's beautiful.

Quick work: Marlow, arm-in-arm with Jilly, walking her down Main Street (paved in copier-paper), slowly, pointing at things, tip-toeing daintily—whoopsy daisy—*It's okay, Jilly, I can fix that, no problem. I can fix that.* Picks her up at arm's length by the waist, carefully carries her outside of the paper city's bounds, sets her down again.

I can fix that.

Flustered, Jilly Zimsky: *I should go.*

I wish you wouldn't

Hm. Well, tomorrow I guess.
Alright, tomorrow.

7

(Day two weekending out at the edge of Calloway's oilfield:
don't tell Mom.)

Leave the wagon in the gully. Jilly Zimsky handholding a
pail full of dark stones. Walk far enough, walk, and then—

8

Marlow abandoning Goliath duties at Calloway's oilfield,
that is, playing hooky with Jilly Zimsky: a matinee movie at
Gibson's Movie House.

What looks good, Jilly?
Anything rated R.
Oh, okay... Uh, and you want cola maybe? Pepsi? And popcorn, too?
*How do you know me like this? Haven't we just met? How do you
know these things about me?*
*I knew your mother, actually. You, dear, are quite new, I would say.
How is your mother, by the way? Has she ever mentioned me before?
She used to call me Marl...*

You can't bring that pail of stones in the theater you know.

Jilly...?
Marl?!

9

MOVIE / BEDROOM ROMANCE SCENE / THREE
MINUTES STRONG PUSHING / NO BLINKING /
INTERRUPTED BY MOVIE CREATURE SPLITTING
CHARACTER'S / AND GUNFIRE / AND GUNFIRE
/ CHARACTERS REDUCED / CHARACTER NOW:

RED PAINT RED WALLS MOVIE BLOOD RED /
CREATURE ON FLOOR / CHARACTER / CRINGING
HOLDING CHARACTER / WET EYES WET FACE
RED PAINT BLOOD MOVIE CHARACTER / OH MY
/ OH MY /
OH /

10
—Credits—
Marlow saying, *Thinking about the creature though, it's amazing. Don't you think?*
Marlow saying, *It's just, I saw the creature's hands; five digits, and, when there was the, ahem, was the close-up flash of the mouth, you know, its teeth, I thought of your mother, the creature losing its limbs and the gunshots, and, your mother, she had a great mouth of teeth, but, is she still ambulatory, after all these years? I—*
Jilly saying, *What do you have to do, Marlow? As a Calloway Goliath?*

Well, slay a bunch of people.
And do you drink the oil?
I don't swallow any, but I do keep a couple ounces in my cheeks just in case.
And the actual Goliath, you being the temporary one or whatever?
Phil Harrison? Real good guy. Adequate giant measurements, too. A real Goliath, Phil. Really good guy.

11
Where have you been all day, Jilly? You smell like oil.
Kiss off, Mama! I can have friends!

12

Jilly Zimsky smiling, unrestrained, filling in her daylight hours with Marl, Marl, equally at ease, except for, in the back portion of his head, where he holds high-schooling memory, dancing, backseating, all that, uncomfortable, a little bit, knowing that, well, this is, in an American sense, uncouth, or unmannerly, not asking her father for, and then what of her mother—*Do you remember me Mrs. Zimsky, Marl?*—unrestrained except for that, but what does Jilly know? Chewing gum, for effect, spitting out and chewing again, newly, for flavor—a new stick—*Them some jaws there, Jilly*, it's working isn't it, *What do you know about it?* Tree breeze romantics, summertime lawnmowers blade-buzzing, and, always, the derricks, churning, distances upon distances of familiar sonorities, likely things, comforting, but how much longer, he thinks, this all being temporary, and if I'm not a Goliath, he thinks, what the happenstance might be, between young Jilly and myself, Jilly Zimsky smiling still, not a care in the world, except for, deep down, somewhere outside of when she is actually with Marlow, Marl, that little tick, switch, inside her head, her pioneer heritage, the simplicity of what it is one does with a Goliath, rocks, and how her mother must have looked, coming home, in high school, with her lipstick everywhere, hair mussed, *Out with that Connors boy again?, Oh, Marl?, That's the one…*

13

Carl, I think you should think about your daughter once in a while. What she's up to. Little missy's out all day, heaven knows where, dirt all over her knees and elbows, and the girl smells like oil, Carl. Oil!
    Okay, yeah, I'll…yeah.

14

Late afternoon, Jilly Zimzky and Marlow cross-legged on the ground looking out at the oil derricks, rotating methodically. Marlow, extending his paper city.

Remember how you called me Marl? Earlier? Keep calling me Marl whydontcha. It's just a fun thing to hear, I think

About your mother, Jilly, I think…
   Don't *ever say* your mother, Marlow.
Jilly Rising; Marlow reaching for her hand. *See me again tomorrow? Please, do come tomorrow. It won't happen again.*

15

Jilly, you smell like oil again. What is going on?!
   Door locked, bedroom: swallowing pills, wincing, swallowing pills. Onset of an episode. Dresses. Jilly trying on every dress. Haste: another one, no another one. Stretching the seams, spent dresses piling mangled on the floor of the closet.
   Jilly, you'll talk to me about this! Open the door! Oil will rot yer brain, Jilly!
   There, the black one. Collapsing into the chair at the vanity, shuddering its wooden frame. Oil-black dress. Oil-black mother pounding on the door.
   Jilly! Jilly, unlock this door! Jilly, please, open the door. Please, Jilly.
   Thinking about his hands around her mother's waist, calculating mother's high school age, how many years ago, and, and
   Carl, can you get up here? She won't open the door.

16

Carl in front of the TV, thinking about the bottom of a lake. Oblivion.

17

Increasingly upset: Jilly Zimsky, face full of house paint: war. Covering wide geographies of freckling. Cheeks. Mania.

Muttering, *Not my mother.*

Muttering, *You, you; I ought; Marl; sonnuva; not no more; not my mother; etc.*

Staring down the mirror in house paint, freckleless, gulping, the record player on, all its volume, woozy, *stop talking about mom, Marl,* tensing, sliding down to the floor, *Jilly…Jilly, can you open this door?* Hair caught around the chair leg, record skipping, *Carl, she won't open the door,* follow the gully, wagon full of rocks (where's his pulse, Jilly?), walk far enough (let's find his pulse)—there: *Hello again, Jilly.*

Summer talk: *Hello, Marlow.*

18

Hello there, Marley, how are things?

*Oh, great, Phil—*you're back.

Sure am. Thanks again for holding down the fort. Them toothaches will turn you over every time, I'll tell ya. Oilfield's lookin' mighty nice, though. And I see you've started a paper replica here.

Ah, yes. They give us the paper so I thought—

Well, you know the paper is for taking notes on oilfield encroachments, right?

Is that it? Oh my, I—

No worries, I'm not a stickler for that type of thing. Anyways, you were just filling in. We can always fill out the paperwork after the fact. And I'll not be shy saying so, it's a marvelous replica. Really good work there, Marley. I'll likely leave it up a few days.

I'm flattered. Thanks.

So, were there any encroachments?

Pardon?

Did you meet anyone approaching the perimeter of the oilfield, and if so, where did you bury them?

Oh, I see, um, yeah, it was fairly slow-going. No, uh, encroachments—that I found. When I was looking.

I would guess not. It's the slow season. Well, here's a statement for your hours. Head over to the Calloway main office and they'll cut you a check. And thanks again, Marley. I'll take care of everything from here.

19

Marlow alone with his check, disoriented slightly in making his way back to town—thinking about Jilly, thinking about Phil. Thinking about, "What now? What do I do now?"

20

JILLY ZIMSKY PUSHING RED PAINT LIPS AT TEMPORARY GOLIATH / (EX-)TEMPORARY GOLIATH / PULL HAIR UP / PUSH-UP BRA / WEAR PENCIL SKIRT / BLACK / WEAR MOM'S JEWELRY / MOM'S NECKLACE / MOM'S RING FOR THAT BLACK / BLACK GOLD LIPS PIONEERING WESTWARD / HAND WAGON FULL O ROCKS / UNATTENDED / TRADING MOUTH OIL / BLACK SMOOCHES / HANDS / KISS / HANDS / MOVIELIKE / KISS / NOT MOVIE / NOT / KISS / KISSING / KISS / KISS / KISS / KISS / KISS / KISS / KISS / KISS / KISS / KISS / KISS / KISS / KISS / KISS

/ KISS / KISS / KISS / KISS / KISS / KISS / KISS /
KISS / KISS / KISS / BREATHE / KISS / BYE THERE
/ BYE / DEAR / DEAR CASUALTY /
MARL /

21

Jilly Zimsky, unknowingly, following that gully path down towards a burial plot—for lack of Marlow; finding Phil Harrison—wagon handle in hand towing Goliath-ready rocks, fist-sized, *I will pioneer you yet, I will, I will, I will, I will, I will;* approaching Marlow's paper community, and Marlow, but not knowing Marlow's being relieved of his temporary position, at Calloway, guarding Calloway's oilfields. That scene.

22

Whoa there, young lady, whoa! Please, just step on back. Yes, step back. This is an oilfield we got here. You'll notice the wells, pointing them out: *there, there, and there…and up over there. So mosey on back the way you came—you don't want to know what I've rights to do.*

    Phil?

    Why, I—as a matter of fact. Now how…do I know you?—wait, those eyes, you're a Zimsky girl, aren't you! I knew your mother.

23
Phil too.

24

Well, I can see where you're coming from. He is much older than you are. Though, love has its ways.

    It's not just that, Phil. He's so nervousy. And he keeps talking about Mom. And I'm a pioneer, so, I'll be moving on anyways. To herself: *I should be moving. Away.*

This is where you live, then? pointing to the paper house.
Yeah. Look, he even folded the back steps and patio. See the creases, there? I mean it's obvious he knows my property pretty well. And you have a basketball hoop in the driveway? Yeah, it's adjustable. Maybe I should maim him a little bit, get the hair out of him. I'm primarily a maimer myself, it's a way to land jobs, but you should follow your heart on that.

You know, Jilly…Jilly, I should probably mention—you say your mom's Jennifer? He's mentioned Jennifer. Jenny, actually. Said they, well…

25

Marlow, cleaned up and nice-looking. Hair combed. Hat to his chest. At the doorstep of Jilly Zimsky and Co.

Ring.

Hello, may I help you. / Uh, hi there. You, uh, you happen to remember me? / Excuse me, wait…Marl Connors? / That's me. / Marl, I've been hearing about you. Have you been outside with my daughter? / I've come to talk with you about that, Jennifer. / There's nothing to talk about, Marl. I mean, if Carl were here—I want you off this porch and out of this yard, you hear me? Out. / Jennifer, please listen to reason. / Out!

26

Poor Phil Harrison, prostrate at the perimeter, a community man, healthy slayer of trespassers, nice goose egg up top on the dome, the temple area, eyes closed, a pile of stones under his chest, a fist-sized stone in his mouth, blocking the air from his throat, as an assurance.

27

Jennifer…Jenny, I've never stopped, I've— / Don't you dare, Marl, don't you even dare keep talking to me. And then, pathetically, *Just, just leave…*

28

Carl, by nature of being Carl, a man married and with a passable interest in his daughter—her livelihood, happiness, what have you—makes his hands make a neck of rope at work, having submerged himself into drinking, car fluids and pills, at Calloway's regional office downtown, standing now, unsteadily, atop his office chair, pressing the weight of himself into his feet into the seat of black leather, to reduce unwanted swiveling, the rope now a tie, backwards, extending towards the ceiling, Carl removing the ceiling tiles in order to get at the ribs of the structure, with the rope, when his secretary walks in, *Mister Zimsky?*, and Carl pausing, before carefully stepping down from his office chair, *Hey Mark, do you mind putting these ceiling tiles back up? I think I'm going to head home for the day.*

Sure thing. Do you still want me to fax out these expense reports?

Yeah, that would be great. Thanks, Mark.

29

Absenting herself, Marlow left at the front door knocking, Carl pulls into the driveway. Rolls down the window,

Marl? Marl Connors?

Hey Carl. How are you?

Oh, you know—just work.

Carl saying something else outside of himself to himself but only inside of his car, not projecting. Gets out of the car. *Anyways, come on inside.* Amiably: *You drink liquids?*

Marlow saying, *Every day, Carl, every day.*

30

Jilly in a frenzy.

31

Guns don't kill people, guns do (they say): the ins-and-outs of lover's mathematics, knives, warring pioneer face paint, rolling a Radio Flyer over paper architecture, wheels tracking and ripping, on principal, after filling Phil's mouth with a stone just small enough to get past his teeth, wood—no evidence—Jilly Zimsky dead in the gully, gone back and without arms, detached, to ensure the blood flow, to the point that they'll wonder if she could've done it herself: she did, raw-throated, sad-eyed, misery painted down her cheeks with pioneering mascara, cursing Marlow, *Marlow!* Latching her limbs in the low strongholds of tightly notched tree branches, first loosening them up with a knife, like the way you can fold paper back and forth along its crease before ripping it, so it comes clean, her arms, clean off, bleeding out, and why, so much so she says it out loud, *Why, Marlow?* Dramatically, having found her paper mother within her paper home, *What is she doing in here?* And, *It's not what you think,* he would've said, though he wouldn't have had to, had he been there, having promised he would be, you ought to keep promises, Jilly thinks, if you're going to disregard paper clothing, as a buffer, paper dolls, I'm only…, and you're, how old are you? *Well,* old enough to know better, but—back in the oilfields, every rock wrenching in the joints of the oil derricks: high black clouds muddy the signal. Poor Phil. And Jilly…

32

Dark smoke visible for miles. Calloway engineers driving Calloway trucks out toward the oilfield. They'll pull the rock from Phil's mouth. They'll step around the mess of crumpled paper. They'll dislodge the stones from the wells. They'll file a report.

33

I'm glad you told me, Marl. She should be home anytime now. The two sitting in the living room, short glasses of liquid in hand, waiting (Mrs. Zimsky upstairs, loading the family pistol).

NEW ANIMALS

We have animals now that are more than animals,

as happens from time to time.

Because animals have what are called 'ANIMAL MOTIVES'.

They're not worried about the blood on their mouths.

Think instead, with these animals

—animals more than animals—

of separating them into limbless steaks, and then you

Will say what you will without fear

HERBERT 2B MAKES A MESS OF THE LOCALS

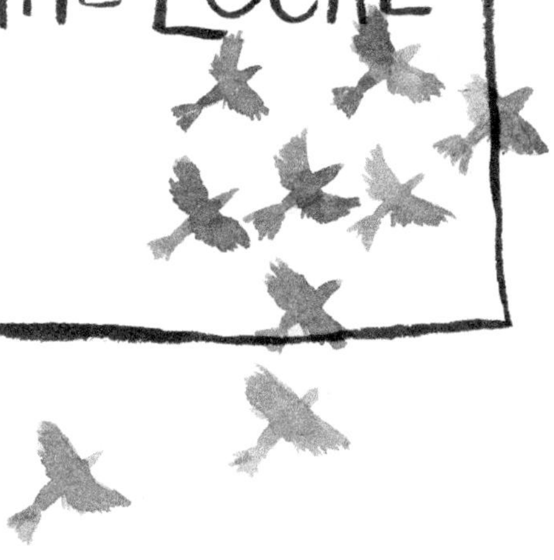

I'll make it important for you to think about that Herbert's in a marriage. First, it's pretty large. You understand what I mean. And it's right to be thinking about equipments when you think about Herbert. About how farming has equipments and kitchens have equipments, because girls now, they're marrying tractors and plows and they're marrying refrigerators—they're marrying microwaves—and things that are Herberts as well are marrying girls. All the time. If you want specifics I'm saying Herbert 2b specifically about marriage with a girl getting married to equipments. My wife. $13,000. Or think about it this way: Herbert 2b is helpmeat, is what she put strung up between us in the marriage so that I might be who I have always have had in me all the time forever what I want to be, but she was a lot of work and marriage is a lot of work and I guess that's why. She's put a full hand of divorces against me already, so we're as much divorced as married now. I suppose this is where Herbert finds his way into marriage with my wife and me. Maybe this helps:

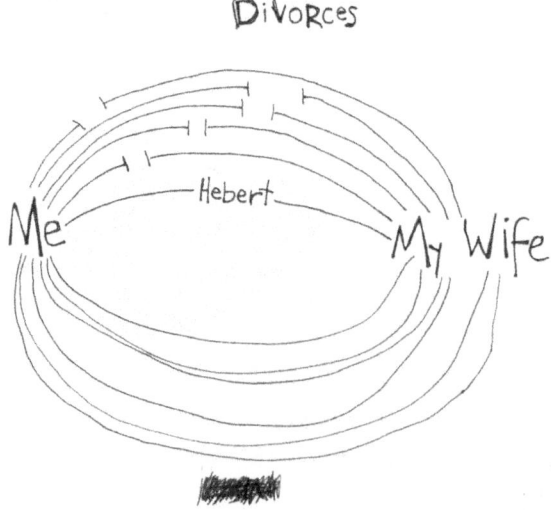

Three's not too large a number I don't think. And equipments, if we think of things in terms of equipments, equipments might do that number down below three and in-between two and three.

I have a small factory all the time in my head. It's what I'm after, it's what I was saying about how I've always wanted to be. A business owner. Two and three-quarters and the marriage is operating all the way fine. Or it was until what Herbert, and let me tell you about Herbert: Herbert is a kind of a moose-like equipment the way it gets through a doorframe, and what Herbert did was make it that we are all out of doorframes—who knew my wife liked the whole set of doorframes so much?—and we can't get upstairs anymore and we're out of the house for groceries and Herbert is still in there and when he put his head down onto the walls it opened things up, the way you could get to any room all at once because every room was the floor now inside of there.

Do you want to know about my wife? I'll tell you in a little bit about my wife who is also now Herbert 2b's wife.

The house then is a station of rubble and all that's left is Herbert mowing down the sticks and beams and everything with his head (equipment) so now my wife, she has me in a hotel and she is in her own hotel not in my hotel and we just left Herbert 2b in the remains of the house. See what I mean? Her: "This isn't the type of thing that is ever working, I'll cut you down straight. Follow?" Me: "Right." Her: "I'll get your throat out of your neck. Follow?" Me: "Right." Her: "Make me think twice I will always do it." Me: "Right." She makes a silly thing at me sometimes and I just have to laugh it off, but I've been hearing worry about Herbert 2b, I really have. Everyone says so.

This will make a spot in your mind: Herbert 2b, inside of Herbert 2b: all birds. Have you been inside a store where birds are everywhere in cages? How it sounds when you are around where Herbert 2b is. What they say in my ears is Herbert 2b has hard feelings is what I mean. No heart. What they say is Herbert 2b has a trumpet for purring out sad purring, he's already within bird-range, and that Herbert 2b's caterwauling that side of town down the drain like a sad sorry Herbert worsting everything that has ears. This, look at this map—I make this—they're saying that Herbert 2b, since we left him, he knocked down this building as well:

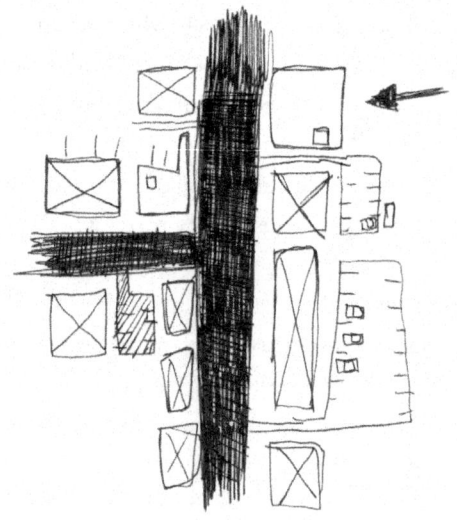

My wife is a wife that will be her own wife, she says this to me, that maybe she is asexual. I have a dictionary. She has cosmetic surgery for her bones that they call her clavicle bones when I'm at the hotel there and I assume Herbert 2b is looking for her and I know where she is, approximately, so I would be looking for her too, if I went out. I could make a business out of clavicle bones. I could make all kinds of businesses. And my wife can use a telephone through imagination, says she might want to cut marriage from her arms and legs and what's still hanging from her back: a marital cape, of sorts, and I think about that. Wait for her: is she going to call?

At one point, what they say—did I tell you about the television?—is Herbert 2b is marching down hellward, digging a moat in circles around and around the old house, still has his trumpet, and is finding all the dead animals that have ever have been dead around the house and making ideas for my wife. But an equipment, whether you want to know about it or not, is not what I'm always going to be when I make a business. Not Herbert.

You understand what I mean.

I have a hard time inside of a hotel but my wife visits me after she has surgery with my money. My money makes new bones for what they call clavicles, for what my wife has in top of her chest just below her neck, what she says are surgical cosmetics. Follow? She'll tell me about what they are and why they flutter, why they jack her up, why she's always carrying and spilling her tea. Where she used to have what are called clavicle bones run two small engine things like hummingbirds is what she has the audacity to say, straight at my mouth, is what she's done with my money. I think it's true. I found it like this:

Different things: I'm right up close to the sun now, for starters. In the hotel again. People are telling me that Herbert 2b is looking around for us. I don't want Herbert 2b to look for me but I want to find my wife since she's always alone from me lately. It's also hard because I'm a future business so I feel terrible that people are calling Herbert 2b bad business and I have him in-between some of my wife and me. They're on the television and they keep telling me that Herbert 2b is all the way in the middle of the city with a bag of dead birds which is ripped and leaking dead birds and filthy animals, not only birds, the insides of birds because of it dragging birds and calling out for the name of my wife and my name, and other animals falling out too: rabbit, mice, possums, tiny hawks, rabbit. It's so much that I pull the covers up over my back and have the pillows on top of my head and ears until the commercial is what is on the television.

A deer's head.

I think where is my wife and Herbert 2b's? Have you seen a cat? I saw this cat for my business and want to know what you think about it for a business and if you think my wife will love me then:

Right?

It's the TV: some downtown artist loves Herbert 2b all the time and kisses his cheeks all the time for art and this is always what I've always wanted to have happen with my cheeks from some rich business magazine and he's not my husband. It's the TV: is enough to tell me that Herbert 2b is big famous and this new artist loves him when Herbert 2b puts his head into how there's a bird picture for the gallery for publicity, I'm upset to kill someone like Herbert because he is so sad for my wife for art.

My wife makes my telephone tell me ringing: "There it is did you see it on TV?" Me: "Uh huh." Her: "He's married to me." Me: "Uh huh." Her: "He's married to you." Me: "Mmmm." Her: "I've got to be off. You understand, don't you?"

It's a good idea to take something with wheels as big as I have for equipments spilling wings and what remains out of a bag—I've done done a decision like this five times before, but this time, come decision-time, I'm gonna have all the gasoline I need to get there—to reduce it—you can hear a store all birds with the door open anywhere—only two minutes before I arrive and I have an automatic car running hard kissing him, 45 MPH, right into a building and making a wreck of it, all metal everywhere, bricks, and some blood bits from my lip, but mostly shrapnel Herbert 2b, buzzard viscera and a burst of feathers like exploding a down pillow, wiry plumes of what my carfront now is a tin flower. You understand. After Herbert 2b seems not to be bird-powered I can get out of the car, carsmoke, and shake people's hands who are looking at us / me, I'm an artist now, a future business, then when I can shake anyone's hand I want I see my wife in the big huddle of lots of lots of people and I get romantic to her through the bodies—I've seen every movie—and give her a little kiss on her hand and hold her hand so that she can't escape, she doesn't seem to, and get one onto her cheek. I'm so much a husband I go select a dry feather to put in her hair and make a position to look eye to eye for the cameras.

Business. Marriage.

OOPS, ISAAC

Cleanly, a seraph may be—in circumstances of less-than-due-diligence, flippant behavior, misfooting, curmudgeonly incident, blinking, shiftless mannerisms, dog marking, princess calamity, turkey-being, asinine speed-travel, shadow casting, misusing of tender fabrics, lock n' chop speaking, dilly-dally, consortium think-balding, lick 'n' smack racketeering, jocular sentiment, consumption, hand slapping, overt savior blocking, miscalculation and general number skewing, personability, feathered brimstoning, cockneyed hip-talking, flaming sword mismanagement, slippery mandibles, and the like—dropped through a cloud.

"You're a good friend, so I won't sit here idly and brick-talk you, Mitchell. It's simple: they're going to pluck you. They're going to pluck you clean."

Morning: under-pillow: 3 x 5 card:
Abraham,

I feel like this has gone on a little long. This Isaac thing. He's a good son, I really think so. The incident with the goats behind the farm and the camel with the rake and the ropes, all of the ropes, the car, and the wheat bushels and the tree branches that were scattered into the house and the water everywhere and what remained of the onion patch was all just a one-time thing. I'm sure of it. I do feel we should let it go. Forgive him? He *is* our son.

Love always,
Sarah

If you lock a seraph down—and let's consider them according to their mythic iconography, embattled wings fish-flapping under the tight weight of rope—and proceed to open the neck, inasmuch as the neck is a door, the contents will be announced, invariably, as a burst of confetti ribbons—that is how seraph's necks open up—and the neck, now hitched and flapping in a manner similar to the jaw (dissimilar to the aforementioned wings), will assume the function of the mouth, modulating speech and, when necessary, coughing. Speaking now takes place doubly, from the crease of the newly opened neck and also, as it had prior to the neck's opening, through the mouth.

Double-mouthed seraphs apologize.

Since the seraph minds its intellectual faculties from the crux of the stomach, the command broadcasts enacting language, flowing towards the mouth from the belly, reaching the new "mouth" (introduced by the opening of the neck) first, followed by an echo transmission from the original mouth. This creates a close-echo speech impediment, or double-speak, that can produce confusion in the listener. Said seraph will then, after the production of a new mouth in the neck, struggle to communicate an admission—what resulted in door-opening the neck in the first place—thereby muddling an atonement. The consequence is, having been denied communion, a diving of the spirit, a withering of the extremities, a clamping of the mouths, a desertion of the spectacle of angelry, and, as it's been so ubiquitously considered, a fall: through dirt, through rock, etcetera, tipping over tableside picture frames, lamps, tablesides.

"What, may I ask, could possibly be the circumstance that puts you here in a chair in my office when I'm usually having my feet in the air over my desk? Do you know about this desk? About why my feet hanging over it is something to consider when you are considering being in my office?

You wouldn't be here. My feet should be up in the air, up over the backskin of my desk, and they're not. My sitting's stifled. Ruffled. So what is it, Mitch? What is it? Mitchell, what is it?"

Angel Mitchell in angel Gabriel's angel office.

"Well, Gabriel, er, I mean Sir Gabriel, sir."

Gabriel, chest-bound in swaths of senior beardliness, flinchless, staring...

Mitchell: "Is it right that the Isaac task was one for the book? I'm assuming? Right, well, do you know, is it already written up? What's to happen; what's happened? Do we have alternates for Isaac, because I think we're down one. We're, uh, down an Isaac, sir. Down an Isaac. We need to redo the Isaac Sacrifice."

A pause.

Then, in a softer tone than expected, "Excuse me?"

And Mitchell, quickly: "Right, we need to redo the—"

"No, I think I heard you. Mitchell, is this for real? We're talking about the Isaac Sacrifice here. Are you messing with me? Mitch, we don't provide redos, Mitch. Mitch, you know this, *you know this.* Where are my feet, Mitch?"

Confusedly: "They're—"

"Where are my feet?"

And then a brief moment before Gabriel continues, "They're under my desk. And we don't do redos and what's this hell you're spitting at me about being *down an Isaac!* Okay, okay, slow up Gabriel"—Gabriel addressing himself, Gabriel gathering himself—"let's take this slow, you can do this." Redirecting: "Mitchell."

Sheepishly: "Yes—"

"What are you telling me?"

Clumsily, cross-stitch-fumbling his fingers: "Okay,

right, uh, yeah, so I'm there—Moriah—and, and, well, it's flowering pretty heavily along the pathway, so Isaac's picking flowers—"

Exhausted: "Mitchell, where are my feet?"

Mitchell, feeling suffocatingly small, squirms silently, dumbly, knows he knows and knows Gabriel knows he knows about the location of Gabriel's feet.

Acknowledging Mitchell's brainworkings: "So let's have at it!"

Startled: "Isaac is dead."

Sound vacuum.

An addendum: "Probably."

Brunch-time: screen door: post-it note:

Abraham,

I'm out behind the tree with Isaac. We have the book and every apple and we're making changes. You're welcome to join. I've spread the large quilt.

Much love,

Sarah.

Also, I washed your summer trousers, so feel free to wear them.

"Probably? Mitchell, my feet…"

"Gabriel, look at it this way, uh…."

"Exactly, Mitch, exactly. I mean, what on earth were you doing that you could possibly have missed it?"

"See, that's just it, I was trying to get the ram's horns tangled in the thicket—"

"What?"

"It's on the itinerary."

Mitchell, removing a folded piece of paper from his right-front pocket, unfolds, reads: "Approximately 10 to 15 minutes in advance of intervention, place ram in northern thicket, interweave horns into portions of solid growth."

"Mitch, it says *10 to 15 minutes ahead of time*, what's the issue here?"

"Have you ever *tried* tangling a ram's horns in a thicket? It's ridiculous! Finding a thicket strong enough is half the battle. And when I finally did locate a thick patch of it, the ram's restless and starts kicking like mad and biting me…

"That and I, well, I was writing a thank you note."

"What?! Mitch, I can't believe I'm hearing this, *a thank you note?* In the middle of the Isaac Sacrifice? You're joking."

"It's just that, well, I really appreciated dinner the other night, your encouragement, and…"

Mitchell looks up: Gabriel, unequivocally irritated, beard shuddering in advance of a seismic shout.

Mitchell interjecting: "I know—your feet."

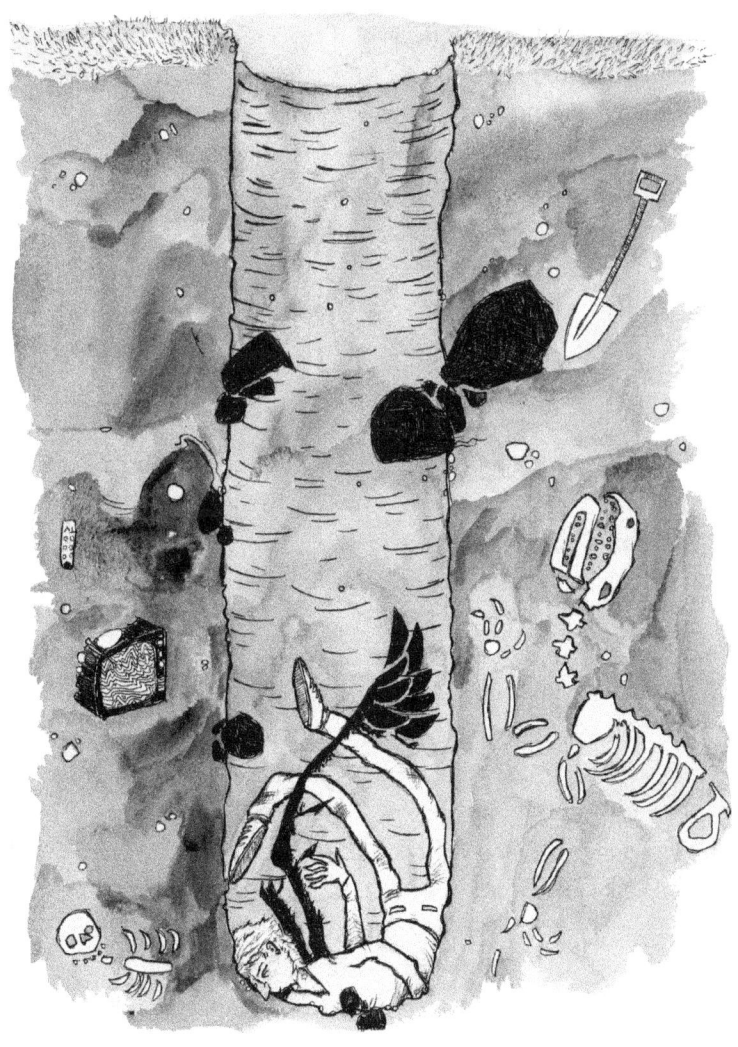

When we review the memory recordings of those asked to sacrifice their solely born, hardwon Isaacs, to ask their sons, full of sacrificial sticks (marrow), to carry the kindling within their shirt, against their skin, to plead with their Isaacs to think abstractly about carrying the kindling against their skin ("But Dad"), their Isaacs having grown bountifully before their eyes over the series of years binding them, originally just a chicken's size, and how they process, once knife deep in an Isaac, their sons, how they think when their Isaac asks about their being a meal for god, and how their skin can be tough, like a goat's, and the technical maneuvering they must purpose in the blade, mixing it between muscles, tendons, cartilage, bones, the subconscious practicality of properly stabbing, and what happens when they turn their mind over the chested splinters from the kindling, mountain-hauled, the skin already tender and pinking red, a trout, a goat, a chicken, for slaughter, when the knife gets stuck, black tributaries thickening outside the bounds previously sealing up any blackness an Isaac might carry, the Isaac desperately question-marking: "Will they eat me, Dad, are they going to eat me?", and flapping, and flapping, under rope, and cawing, despite trying to be dignified, for their father, what that does, and when the serrated portion of the knife locks on a notch of bone, the should-have-been-attendant angel then appearing, visibly dejected, reproachable, shoulders tilted in a manner expressing failure, onlooking, and whether or not this is comprehended, in the moment, for what it is, and if, among the duration of the recording, upon review, there is a hint at what purpose the angel might have had, it having appeared and then promptly disappearing, in the midst of the hitched blade, a fading son, a lonely red mountain top, a sonless father—when we review the tapes our findings are inconclusive.

Selections from the Abrahamic Recordings Archive:

(11:31) This, I have this, this, the knife's here, do I have everything? Keys? Wallet?

(12:06) Where the—Where is he going? *Back over here!* *Isaac! Isaac!* I swear, that kid's as loose-brained as a donkey, wandering after flowers. Flowers for heaven's sake! He's making a mockery of this. This is supposed to be about him. Or me? What is this? Walk, Abraham, just walk. All in god's time. All in god's time.

(12:21) I don't understand, isn't it that I'm not supposed to—the boy is sweating so hard now. Isaac's always been good, as dumb as he's been. Always good. An obedient son. Like me. Like me...Father?

(12:34) Sarah...Sarah, I...

(12:35) *Just wrap it under your shirt, boy!* The boy's never been this way. He knows. No. It's just a shirtful of sticks. And he's fine, strong enough. Serves him though, if he's to talk back to me. Maybe this is the right thing for him if he's turning that way—

(12:57) Sarah. What will she say? What am I going to tell Sarah? What should I tell Sarah? Oh Sarah. Oh Sarah. Sarah, it's just that, that. Oh god—

(13:14) *God will provide a sacrifice, dear boy, god.* Oh father god, please please please please please please please please please please please please please please please please please

please please please please please please please please please
please please please please—

(13:36) Sweet Sarah, please forgive me.

(13:44) Why won't this kn- kni- kn- this kni- kni- *Almost, boy
no no no* this knife dammit, *Almost* like a burnt chicken this
kid—god?—this kniii—

(14:00)

OFFICIAL REPORT: ISAAC SACRIFICE
REPORT NO. 998553221824139413932211777
SUBJECT: Mitchell
CIRCUMSTANCE: Tardiness in the last-minute halting of
Abraham's commanded sacrifice of Isaac.

COMMENTS: The council will note ineptitude in terms of
angelic monitoring and intervention regarding the subject,
Mitchell IV, and his mismanagement of Abraham-and-Isaac
with relation to Abraham's commanded sacrifice of Isaac.
The operation states specifically: pre-sacrifice arrival and
audible announcement, "Psych!" It is suspected/assumed
Mitchell IV suffered hereditary mental lapsing common of
angel Mitchells in relation to his assignment to intervene. Be
that as it may, it is inexcusable that the knife landed in flesh.

SUGGESTIONS: Candidly, it is widely the opinion of
seraphim familiar with Mitchell IV that Mitchell IV is
hopelessly incompetent, slovenly in appearance, given
to rapid eye movement even when awake, a habitual

rubbernecker, portly hearted, frequently dressed in off-white robes, permeating a mustard-like scent, in need of a new comb, stumble-happy, late with thank you notes, a poor swimmer, consumes white bread, has poor taste in contemporary music, and is therefore not representative of the office of Abrahamic Intervener. That being the case, some do suggest compassion in circumstances of penitence: I suggest a sheer drop.

Evening: front door: scrap-paper adhered with scotch tape:
Abraham,

I left a blueberry pie to cool on the windowsill in the kitchen. It's under a cloth. You and Isaac should have some. Sorry, I'm a little sleepy so I'm going to bed early.

Yours,

Sarah

When considering double-mouthed apologies, or seraphic apologies in any measure, always remember to reduce the volume of the expression by quilting the mouth(s) over with the skins of winter-coated mammals. Celestially speaking, apology is the loudest form of utterance. Make considerations for your angelic neighbors—whether corporate or suburban— by hunting, gathering and stitching now, in advance of any instances of apology that occur outside the bounds of omniscience. It has been known to happen.

To hard-muffle a contrite seraph is to perform mediation on behalf of The Most High—to succor both the penitent angel and the celestial community at large.

Seraphs operating in close range of celestial apology have reported a slow and steady disintegration of the inner ear (the debris of inner ear appearing visibly as ash-colored dandruff settled in the crevices of the ear canal and atop the shoulders) resulting eventually in deafness to godly communications of the audible variety. Afflicted seraphim are encouraged to collect the disintegrated fragments of their inner ears for waste disposal and apply for a light ear-boxing provided by god's hands.

Remember: apologies should always be directed to god. Apologies otherwise addressed constitute apostasy, and, as such, demand the immediate withdrawal of seraphic standing, i.e., immortality. Said seraphim—though, no longer seraphim—will experience mortal death and be removed to outer darkness.

"I'm sorry Mitchell, it's regulations."

"Sarah."

"Abraham. What time is it?"

"Sarah, I—"

"No, don't apologize. I'm on your side now. This afternoon when we were out with the apples—I thought you'd be out there with us though (did you get your trousers?)—Isaac was acting strange. It was an odd number of apples, sure, but that he went ahead and ate an advantage over me—without a word, mind you—it was enormously impolite.

"Also, we were making some changes to the book—you read my note, right?—I was working the odd-numbered pages, he the even, and when I look over, all he is doing is drawing: superhero characters and comics, all over the revelations—though, I think you will be happy with what I've done: I've let loose from the iambic and also doled out some very assertive line breaks—but back to Isaac: I correct him and all he does afterward is mope and write notes in the margins—and they're all addressed to the Jordan girls. The Jordan girls! How does he even know the Jordan girls? Well, I think we put our foot down, put an end to it right now. I don't mind if the two of you already had at the pie tonight, we can talk it over with him in the morning.

"Where is he by the way, did you already send him to bed? I didn't hear the sink running, did he brush his teeth?

"Abraham?"

"Sarah, I…"

"Where's Isaac?"

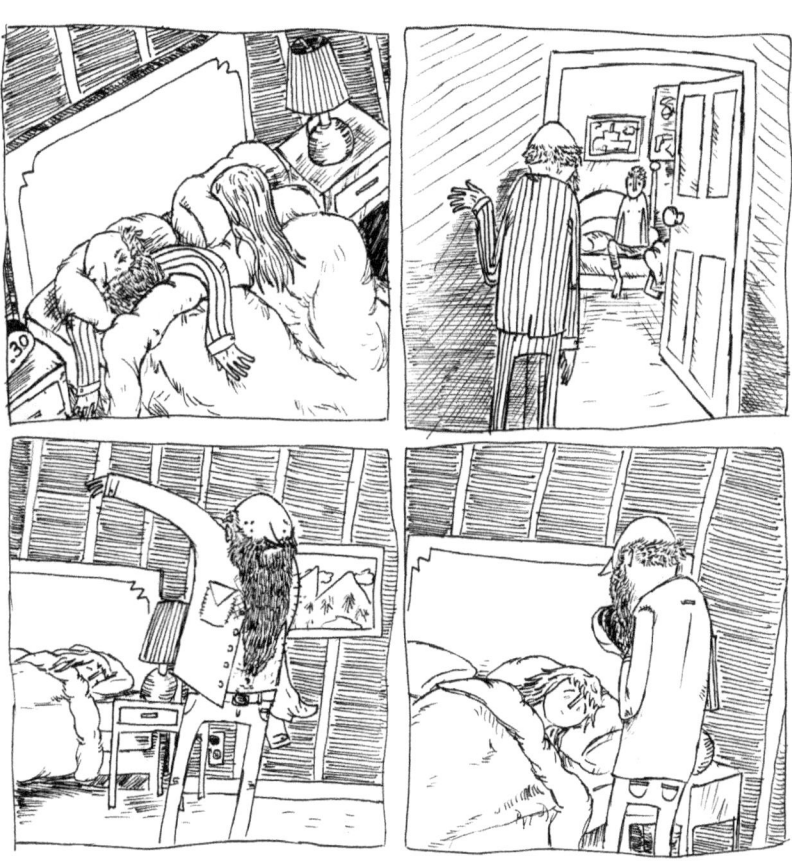

If it wasn't for the megaton slippedy-slip, this one might not be against the floor, jowls loosened, face: a mishmash of tender under-eye skin, flapped over soggily—the dime-work of what the winged beast has called, 'flipping the wrong pancake'—netted wing-wings feather-worried in bird wire, a bit wet in the formal area, tennis sneakers all scuffed—no longer of the clouds.

But just as well, you need to know this part too. Where it all goes.

Left: golden variety bones, ringing sonorously. The mandible, teeth removed and laid out in diagram by centimeters, a wingflap constellation connected by pencil lines. Vertebrae in a wreath. Ribs middling the wreath in a crosshatch (loosely connected where broken/shattered). A healthy steam rising.

Right: wing 1, wing 2, wing 3, wing 4. Angel-layer skin and second skin, both severed and flat for sunning purposes. Baby teeth, formed in the neck/second mouth. Lungs (if intact, these may still hold fish). Cuticle areas. Muscles found in the bicep and thigh areas. Other muscles. If unshattered: eyes. Assorted angel viscera, in wax paper. Inner-angel smell. Etcetera, etcetera.

After midnight: kitchen parlor, table: loose stationary:
I'm going to get the body. Don't bother coming. I have my plans.

Broken,
Sarah

A selection / thread from the Sarah Recordings Archive:
(00:02) it's dark-ocean skies ocean-dark skies it's too warm
out here the temperature's too warm for him to be dead out
here much too warm too pleasant why is it so nice out how
can it feel like this out here if he's dead out here if there's
blood what kind of god shouldn't the moon be red shouldn't
the stars be tearing away from the sky holing it up exposing
that contemptible one-way mirror room I can imagine
them there their bulbous deformed heads curious eager
animalistic peering down on me right now they're peering
down on me you're peering down on me your subject your
game piece accounting for me like dumbfounded curious
children younger than my son younger than Isa...Isaac
like Isaac...Isaac in my arms this morning Isaac *Isaac!* I I
can't keep this pace need to need to gut up need to gather
it's so warm out so nice out here Isaac even if the moon
isn't falling on my head isn't bleeding on my gown even the
earth if the earth wants to sleep wants to purr and yawn
and stretch the way it is stretching out my path like a cat
cats even in this darkness *it's too beautiful tonight, too beautiful
a night, not tonight, not my son dead, not tonight* my son can't die
tonight he's alright I know he's alright he wouldn't let him
go let him go I was just cradling him cradling his head this
morning and the groceries the milk Abraham if you can do
one proper thing you put that milk away put that damned
milk away Abe I won't have my baby coming home to retch
at that milk and me neither with this god giving only one
not more than one son hands feet wrists tiny ankles Isaac
he needs his mother me soft hands I need my boy and he a
father who hasn't killed him who hasn't bowed low to some
infant god Abraham what were you thinking look at this
look at what you've done to Isaac what in the world could

you get some water from the well I Said Get Some Water From The Well Abraham it's no longer your charge he's my son he's my son it's so damned warm out he's my son he's my son he's my…where is he where are you Isaac I can't see there there's Moriah I can get there I can make it *Isaac, wait up honey! Momma's coming!* Gonna take care of you sweetheart Momma's coming Momma's gonna take care of you god wants you to stay with me now god's with you sweetie just hold on what am I saying god please god let him be there let him be okay god please I need my boy Isaac I need Isaac this this can't be happening this didn't happen he's back in bed maybe I should go back this isn't real this couldn't actually have happened no it's okay Isaac Momma's coming this is all a test just a test god I'm faithful lord please forgive me please it's just I love him this boy so much lord the poor boy I'm sorry I know I've loved him more than you I'm sorry but I'm honest I have honesty that boy lord I need to see his eyes feel his skin warm see breath move his chest understand understand that you are destroying me this will destroy me sweating my dear I'm sweating keep walking Sarah it's your boy up on top of this mountain he needs you how can it me so warm how can you let my child when stupid stupid Abraham can't look at Abraham's face again after I'll shatter him can't go back can't I god kill me right here if he's dead send your wolves tear me limb from limb whatever this is god whatever…whatever it is…whatever is for me up here give me strength lord forgive me almost breath okay go

"What, what is this?"

huff
huff

Undone and only, Isaac lies awake, a flush of wind, buttery, up and down his chest, chest crusted over in redness, red-crusted into the grass off next to the altar, the altar hiding him from view, and the ram, still shuffling, kicking, and lurching, though limply, to loosen its horns from the bramble. A gurgle, softly, bubbling up in the neck, as Isaac, paralyzed, lies, shirt torn and warm to the wind walking into his newly opened areas—there being many—eyes blinking, slowly, blinking—is that all that's not paralyzed?—before the earth's gravity competes, momentarily, with the gravity of the heavens, lifting the lonely body of the slow-blinking Isaac an inch or two from the ground, as he is marked by a scope of light pillaring around him, a column, speaking down to him from heaven, as his mother is carrying off something else—another son, he thinks. He hears: "Looks like he's still mostly intact, Gabriel. Do you want me to separate him?" And Gabriel, apparently, "No, leave that to me. I'll pull him apart myself."

She has the body and she's dragging it back home, confetti trailing out from the neck behind her. It's too heavy for cradling, coddling, its wings singed black, chopped, and Sarah muttering, renaming it her firstborn in confusion. She uses her back for lifting. The weight of celestial bodies exceeds that of terrestrial bodies. She uses her back, mostly, not her legs, knowing that she'll not have legs for legging with, across the prairie, the biblical grasses, if she uses only her legs; and it's almost morning. And if someone emerges they might ask how, dear Sarah, is your good son, Isaac?

"S——, Sarah? What is this? Who?"

"Abraham, this isn't about you anymore. I'm taking Isaac upstairs. Set the door open with the doorbrick and move out of the way."

"Sarah…that's, that's not Isaac, Sarah. What—what are you carrying?"

Glares that bore holes are glares that bore holes. Abraham, literally, though invisibly, takes a hole through his chest from Sarah's glaring. Something is carved through him, whether physically or religiously, whatever it is, and he falls back.

"Where's the duct tape? He's leaking confetti out of his neck."

Choking sounds, Abraham down on the floor now, holding his chest, unable to look upward from the pain. "S-S-Sar-keh-k-Sara—"

"Okay fine, I'll find it without you. You just go on lying there. You've done enough already."

"S-S-krrg-uf-Sa…"

Early morning: unmade bed: half-torn notepaper, Sarah's side, discarded:

Dear Sarah,

    I

Gabriel, turning over Isaac: Now, the wings should—*the wings?* Pulling Isaac's face from the ground by the hair, sideways, so as to open his mouth, check his molars— Why, this isn't...Gabriel, looking in each direction, sees the ram, ram-horned into the bramble and sleeping, exhausted, head hanging up awkwardly in the thicket, body slumped beneath in a wearied heap. And then, scanning the mountaintop, the pit. A hole bored into the earth's surface. Twenty paces or more from the altar place—and the body, here, in his arms: Isaac?

When handling torn human frames with angelic fingers, invoke pretense in every grip. Invoke the almighty for approval, informally, through prayer—and proceed. Reduce the thighs, as is necessary, the hips, before hoisting about the shoulders—as a lamb—though, first, slap the cheeks heartily. Still alive? Confuse the muscles into waking. Death is not death—the messiah—reversals requiring, however, of course—(*of course)*—paperwork. Spiritual submissions for approval. Resurrecting being the consideration of the most high and a necessary condition of his eternal plan/ planning—better to avoid, if possible, undue bureaucracies, salvaging the working parts in a manner that's operable. Address the wounds with hands aglow. Seal the flesh.

And nourishment. Bless the ram. Feed him the ram.

Early morning: pit-bottom mud: thank you card:
Dear Gabriel,

Thank you—particularly for everything. All of it. I tell everyone this, but you're a good friend. Truly.

All the best,

Mitchell

Propped up at the table, though stooping forward, eyes nearly closed, but not quite.

"Isaac has grown, hasn't he?" Sarah, whisking something together for breakfast, breaking eggs while heating the stovetop.

In his mind: That's not Isaac, dear.

Abraham, down against the open door, motionless, colorless, hand holding the invisible hole in his chest, and sweating in the morning sunlight. There is confetti everywhere, eternally, on the linoleum floor, and spread throughout the halls of the house, in the bedrooms, and tucked into the furniture—funneling and playing outside even, carrying in the low-lifting breeze.

Faintly: "Sarah, check there, look-k at his back, that's not I-Isaac. See the…those stumps? This is anuh-hkkg," he swallows, "another thing altogether. Just look at at how its m-mouth hangs there, Sarah. I d-don't think it's, I don't think it's human. Sarah, it's—"

Sarah sends the skillet, half-heated, flying across the kitchen at Abraham, missing, instead chipping a notch out of the wood of the door, just above his head, the skillet rebounding into the floor, spinning atop and melting some confetti into the linoleum.

Mitchell lifting, with all his strength, his eyelids, up, up, a centimeter or so, looking down, at the skillet.

"*Don't* you talk about Isaac anymore, Abraham! Not one word! Don't you talk to Isaac."

Heat the ram with the palms of your hands. Using the middle finger, cut away and discard the skin. Serve. Boys are in need of nourishment when without food for an extended period of time and suffering gaps in the flesh, in the stomach, chest, and neck, particularly when inflicted by their fathers. Of necessity, manipulate the ram muscle into a mush or paste, again using the hands—heating and reducing—before offering, or rather, force-feeding, if he—the boy—is unresponsive. If all else fails, consider chewing the meat into something swallowable. Birds do this. Enflame the tongue to avoid the taste of flesh. How dead is he? You will want to generate this thought. Death is an abstract placed along a continuum: How dead is he?

Abraham, unsettled by Mitchell, tries again: "Sssarah, p-please, it it's n-not Isaac."

Sarah walks over to Abraham. She bends down and with great effort pulls Abraham up from the ground, hooking her arms around his waist. The strain of doing so, and the momentum of Abraham lifting upward when Sarah jerks, sends Sarah's back against the wall and a picture frame falls to the ground. Once she's steadied him, she pushes him towards the door, supporting him from collapsing again, shoving him out through the doorframe. He lands in a pile of himself, his right shoulder and arm underneath the bulk of him awkwardly.

"You're not Abraham."

And she closes the door.

"It's okay, Isaac. My name is Gabriel. You will be sorted out. We will sort you out. This was a mistake and…well, this was not supposed to happen, we don't usually have mistakes like this, but I'm going to take care of you—restore you, so to speak."

Gabriel fist-cooking ram and inserting it into Isaac's stomach.

"I apologize, I do. You will receive a formal written apology from me shortly, so let's make sure you have the opportunity to read it in a mortal capacity, shall we? Isaac? Come on now Isaac, lets take a look through those eyes of yours."

Isaac lying on his back, stone-faced, eyelids fallen open but offering no recognition.

Sarah—Abraham gone—stands with her back to the backdoor, unmoving, feeling at the emptiness and the newly resonant silence generated by Abraham's absence. Utilizing what she can of every sense she has left—the feeling in her flesh, the hollow within her ears, the lingering syrup-stained air, and what saliva she holds in her mouth—Sarah absorbs the solitary feeling of what she understands, what she tells to herself, is the post-Abrahamic era. Only a thin wooden door and the length of a metric yard separates her from her husband the prophet, crumpled in the backyard grass, she indoors and he out, yet her resoluteness, the remembered action of Sarah unloading the dead weight of Abraham's glare-scored body, has introduced unforeseen movements within her head. She remembers and remembers the unloading, as if the action had taken place outside of herself, as a means of driving home the reality of her doing what thing she had done. When she has convinced herself of herself, Sarah stands, absorbing the cavity-feeling of her newly emptied home, Mitchell collapsed still atop the kitchen table, and says to herself, There is no going back. A former self encourages Sarah to recognize her triumph, but she maintains the alterations within her—her new self—and accepts no triumph in this. Standing still, Sarah, her eyes open, glittered over and glazing with oncoming tears withheld, feels a hulking within her chest, in her lungs and heart, feels the follicles on her arms and shoulders, spreading down her back, hips, and legs, standing themselves, alert to the soundlessness, before the fire alarm chirps, the battery in need of changing. She stands, the twenty-four or more previous hours of her experience collapsing on top of her, arriving in large chunks, connecting and filtering and consuming her with the recognition of this pivot-point that she's arrived at, this course-bending in the trajectory of her life.

She makes her first move towards the refrigerator, drinks lemonade directly from the carafe. She places the carafe back in the refrigerator and looks down at Mitchell.

Isaac.

She forgets everything and sits down at the kitchen table.

Abraham, decamped.

Abraham, missing a hole-sized portion of himself, lying on the grass.

Abraham, lying on top of himself on the grass, his right shoulder positioned in a manner that means it's out of its socket.

Abraham, opening his eyes underneath himself, looking back at the backdoor of his home through the invisible hole in his chest, sighing as a means of breathing.

Abraham.

Brunch time: kitchen door glass: copier paper with scotch tape:
Dead Abrahams Only

Sarah blinks. She stands and walks over to the body laid out atop the kitchen table. She takes hold of one of the ashen stumps protruding from its back, gripping it enquiringly. She lets go, stands, looking over the body. She traces her fingers along the spinal cord until she reaches the base of the neck and there pulls lightly at tufts of the brown-blonde hair. With one hand she allows the hair to course through her fingers, sensing the scale of the skull. She touches the skin of the profile of face that is visible, probing it lightly, gently, casually testing its pliability. She doesn't crouch to peer, but remains standing upright. She pulls up the upper lip and examines the teeth. She brushes a stray confetti string from the table. Now she crouches, running her hand along the throat of the neck until she reaches an opening, like overly wide lips, at its center. She feels at the opening, sensing the circulation of air—breathing. Sarah stands upright again. She opens the eyelid facing her. The eye holds still, or almost still, however, holding the eyelid open, she watches the eye slowly—slower than seems human—fix itself to her, making eye contact. She holds the eyelid open for a half-minute longer, then let's go, letting her hand drift back to her side. Maintaining eye-contact all the while, the eyelid closes again, ever so slowly. Staring down at the body for a moment longer, Sarah silently excuses herself, entering the connected living room and laying herself onto the couch.

Gabriel holding Isaac in his arms. Isaac doubly opened, by Abraham, by Gabriel, and finally, within the struggle of digesting angel-cooked ram meat, ceases breathing, ceases having a heart beating, even faintly. Gabriel rocking Isaac in his arms, humming softly, almost inaudibly. Isaac no longer Isaac in his arms, but Isaac's body in his arms, being rocked. Gabriel holding Isaac, stands, walks over to the angel-pit bored into the ground by Mitchell's falling and unceremoniously drops Isaac in, Isaac's body thudding weakly. Gabriel stands over the pit, if only for a moment, sees Mitchell's note next to Isaac, reads it (angel eyes), then wanders off, no longer humming.

Sarah, asleep on the couch.

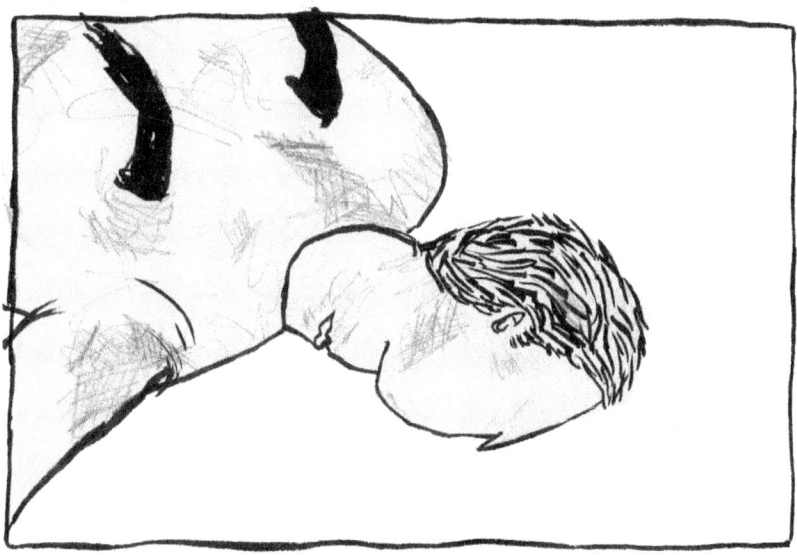

He (by which it's meant god) will allow, on occasions when grief is overwhelming, a seraph to take leave; occasionally. To remove itself from the heavenly catalog. To miss roll call. To think itself unseen, circumstances requiring/permitting. To unravel, to loan out its organs, to misappropriate seraphic glory, to adopt, to shudder with doubt, to be consumed in fire, to misunderstand holiness, to cloud with anger, to make savior movements, to entertain self-destruction, to desire, to retrace wingflaps, to make art, to cast shadows, to enjamb scripture, to allocate arm strength to the clipping of wings, to sell dental fillings, to grow tired, to grow weak, to grow absent, to pose questions, to be reasonable, to fill with blood, to fill with regret, to set bushes on fire, trees, grass. To weary. To weep. To handle the knife edges of a splintered stone. To think.

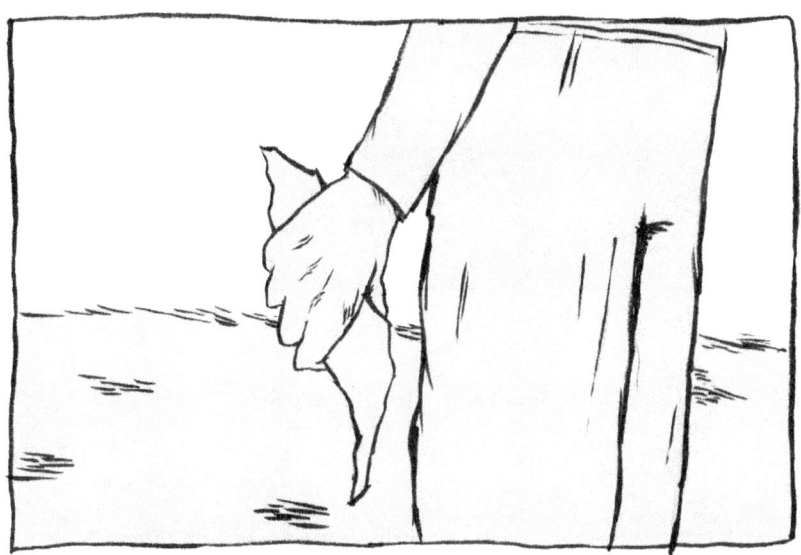

Abraham, empty of the portion of himself opened by
Sarah's glare, makes himself stand. Standing takes every
effort; takes forever. Abraham walks to the tree in the
backyard. Walks further, wandering, into rocks, trees, cars,
shrubs, farmyard, looking for the lord—"Are you there,
lord?"—speaks with the god of rocks, the god of trees, the
god of cars, shrubs, farmyards, wandering, mind mottled
with half-thoughts and debris, ambling into anything,
everything, clumsy, a small stone, a bush, talking to god, a
bush, or searching for him, asking, asking, gets disoriented,
finds a shovel, begins to dig and dig and dig and dig and dig
and dig and dig and dig and dig and dig, digs a hole, a pit,
gets inside his new hole, his pit, is inside his new pit digging,
talks to the god of the pit, talks to himself, listens to the pit,
prepares for sleep, prepares for something he tells himself
is sleeping, prepares for closing his eyes and not opening

his eyes and to be thought sleeping, whether or not it is the case. Abraham looks upward, through the hole-opening, the hole in his chest throbbing. Looking down on him is his son, Isaac. Isaac waves. Abraham closes his eyes.

Gabriel's mind rewiring in the act of retrieving Mitchell from the kitchen table and returning him to the hole— Isaac and Mitchell—before and after, continually, Gabriel's mouth doubling in his neck, reregistering past, present, and future—Gabriel:
(∞) There is actual darkness.

She will wake up thinking, Isaac?, and will look back over towards the now-empty table. She'll say, Okay, softly, and sit up. She will look about her, about the silence of her empty home. She will stand up and walk slowly around the room, her hand tracing against the walls, and into the kitchen, touching the chairs. She will open the backdoor, look out into the open space, the air. She will see the tree under which she had, only a day earlier, eaten apples with her son. She will stand there, staring at the tree from a distance. She will think about chopping the tree down. She will not approach the tree, however. No. She will re-enter her home.

Carved into the backyard tree:
Dear, dear Sarah,
    I'm sorry.
    A.

WINIFRED,

NOT A HORSE

1

I have a good friend named Winifred, but I won't use that as an excuse. No, I don't have a problem with that. If you want a horse's name, have a horse's name. I'm not named Winifred, that's not my name. But Winifred, yes, she is named that way and she has that excuse, I suppose, if she needs it. And she may, that's not my place. She is who she is. A part of that is Winifred sees things differently through her glasses, I can tell. Dimly, hazy. That is, she wears these glasses that she wears and it's obvious she doesn't like to see, or—excuse me—*she doesn't have good vision.* I do my part to do what I can to know someone, Winifred in particular, and so I have it in me to have glasses that are Winifred-glasses, or glasses that make an experience of how Winifred sees things. What I figured out is that looking through Winifred's glasses, or using her eyes to look through her glasses (I've done my research), is like looking through a sheet of vellum paper. To get to understand this better, I walk around one day holding a sheet of vellum paper in front of my face. It helps me understand my good friend named Winifred and how she gets where she's going, which is a miracle. Try walking around holding a sheet of vellum in front of your face, I tell you. Winifred-glasses. But once I understand this fact, that my good friend Winifred walks this way, as if in a sea of vellum, with her large glasses, I lay on the sidewalk a few paces in front of her—perpendicular, not crossways. She falls on top of me because she can't see through her glasses and she says, My goodness, a horse. I find this funny because Winifred's a horse's name and I'm not a horse, but Winifred, aside from falling on top of me and thinking I'm a horse, or saying so, she has a meadow of horses behind her tall house that's a grey house. You would think a witch lived in the house if you've ever been to Salem, because in Salem they try to convince you about witches, and they work pretty hard to get a hysteria going, but I wasn't buying it when I was there. Anyways, since she calls me a horse, or because she says, My, what a horse you are, and fumbles around with my blouse there on the ground—we are both on the sidewalk—I don't tell her it's me. I simply neigh at her and she says, Shondra?, which I think is one of the names of one of her horses. I know this because I often stand behind her while she is in her meadow of horses and she has one out there she's named Shondra, and then four others with the names Madeline, Hefner, Bimmers, and Cynthia—five horses in all. When I neigh again, she says, Shondra, what are you doing lying on the sidewalk? And we both get up, but I get up on my hands and knees because I don't want to give myself away. It's then Winifred, my good friend, she climbs onto my back and says, We might as well head home, and it takes two hours for me to crawl to the bus stop with her riding me and then I neigh-talk Winifred onto the bus. When I follow the bus on foot, jogging, keeping an eye on Winifred, the bus stops not too far from where it was when I neigh-talked Winifred onto it a couple blocks behind me, and she gets out. We are pretty close to my apartment, so I gather her up and into my apartment using my Shondra disguise of walking on my hands and knees, because Winifred is obviously confused. And there she is, I have her in my apartment. (I can't say I haven't always wanted Winifred in my apartment. I just can't say that.) When we are in my apartment I use the bathroom to wash my hands and knees which I've scraped and bloodied along the sidewalks while under the weight of my good friend Winifred, who, despite her horse's name, is fairly petite (though I've never carried someone on my back before, petite or otherwise). Winifred sits on my couch for a while just staring forward pleasantly and we kind of look at each other—her through her glasses and me through my vellum paper. Eventually I tell her, Winifred, it's nice to have you over but I want to use the television, and she tells me that it's been a while and have I seen Shondra around? And I say no while I'm escorting her out of my building, because it's getting late and Winifred should know better, I don't care how old she is.

2

I don't use the vellum paper anymore, or at least I don't use it to try and see what is happening on the television, because when I look into Winifred's windows I can't see a television anywhere and there is no need for me to see what it's like to be my good friend Winifred watching television when she doesn't own a television set. That's common sense. When I'm over at her house, I look out to her meadow and I can see Bimmer eating grass and I realize that horses are smaller and hairier than I thought because he's right up close to the horse fence. I know Winifred won't mind, because of our close relationship, so I open up the horse fence and I see what I can do with this horse she has, Bimmer, since the other horses are a ways off in the meadow and I can work with Bimmer one-on-one, which is my specialty. I feel disappointed by the fact that Bimmer is willing to bite my hair and drag me a few feet before screaming something, which when a horse screams they call it whinnying. I'm disappointed because I feel like it's cliché to have your hair bitten by a horse and I don't even bother to stop in and say hi to my friend Winifred who I came to see if she had a television for sure because I'm feeling deflated and my hair has been one of my best qualities, I've always thought, but that didn't stop Bimmer. And so it is. I go home and watch a television show about a horse who is also a painter, to relieve the tension I feel about Bimmer and horses, and that not all horses fit within a box of horse traits the way Bimmer is trying to convince me about horses.

3

It becomes easy for me to have Winifred invited as a tagalong guest to things when I explain that Winifred isn't a horse. My friends, for example, they invite me to dinner and I ask them if my friend named Winifred can come and they ask me to describe her and I tell them to imagine her in a small red coat and with glasses, and when they think about it, they know that there are no coats that are made big enough for a horse to fit in them, and then they consider, even if a coat was made big enough for a horse, how difficult it would be to get the horse's hooves and legs into the sleeves and they can easily see that Winifred is not a horse. I also tell them about Winifred's glasses and how she can't see well and that, for her, seeing is like looking through a sheet of vellum paper and I bring over sheets of vellum paper so they can understand her better. These details seem to convince them that there is no way Winifred is a horse. Though, when at last I say, She is not a horse, that makes it conclusive, and things proceed. I know because when we have the dinner, Winifred's there. She's easy to recognize. At dinner I can tell that Winifred likes eating meat because when she has the meat in her mouth she takes a long time eating it and chews a lot because she is savoring it and I watch her chew and chew, which is easy to do without feeling self-conscious because for Winifred, seeing me across the table is like seeing a blob of human-shaped color. I'm not even sitting across from Winifred, I'm sitting next to her, so that even makes me even more inconspicuous to Winifred when I'm watching her chew her meat. I realize, however, while watching my friend Winifred jawing at her meat, that my friends who invited me and told me that I could bring Winifred are looking at me looking at Winifred and they are screwing up their faces and making silent, confused gestures with their heads and eyes. They are looking back and forth between me and Winifred in a way that seems equivalent to saying something like, You know, Winifred is not the only one who deserves to be watched chewing meat, or, more likely, Why are you watching Winifred eat her meat?

4

I didn't know how hard it was or how long it would take to kill a horse until I had to kill Winifred's horses in order to keep her in supply of meat. I've done the research, and around here it's not easy to find grass-fed meat. But I knew how much she loved meat after dinner, I knew it, and I was worried about whether or not she would have enough, or the possibility that she didn't get enough, which would explain her eating all the meat at dinner. I haven't yet talked to my friends about having my friend Winifred over for dinner, because after she'd finished eating the meat I thought it was best to get her home and I excused the both of us, so I can't say what the impression was. I am prepared to tell them, however, that it's difficult to make small talk when you're eating meat and that's probably why Winifred didn't talk as much as they might have wanted her to, and how did they like her dress? I mention the dress, or I plan to, because it was light purple and I think it's a good diversion, because I'm not interested in sticking up for Winifred when she can do it herself, and the dinner seemed undercooked, the way Winifred had to chew at it. When they get back to me, or I see them, we'll talk, but I thought it more important to get Winifred the meat she needs, I can tell, and so, as I said, I had to kill the horses. And so far as that goes, I'm not shy about saying that horses' necks don't break easily and if you want to break the neck of a horse, make sure you have enough rope and some stamina, and that the tree branch you're using, or trunk, whatever you've got for leverage, is set near you once you've cinched the neck-knot. I didn't do this and the first horse was just dragging the rope around the field. It ended up that the old well behind Winifred's house that is falling apart, the loose bricks from the well, those can be used to wear the head of a horse down enough that you can stop it and make use of it if you're friend's in need of meat. Winifred. And not only the head, I should specify, that's just where you need to direct your aim. And even then, I didn't know how long it was or how hard it would be to kill all the horses, and I found that even after I had used every loose brick, I had to reuse the bricks in order to get the effect I was going for: a fixed heap of horsemeat. I should say that, after things started going the way I wanted, or getting there, I'd only downed one horse, not all of them. I love horses. And while I'm not sure if that's enough meat to keep Winifred happy, I think it will keep her fed for at least a week. And a royal week of horsemeat is enough. She's getting up there agewise. No need to waste the horses, even for a friend. Though now I have to figure out what to do about butchering, since that is something I'm new to as well. The other horses are whinnying from across the meadow, looking in this direction, and I wonder what it means to be a horse and to have a horse roommate be horsemeat food, because all animals are food. The horse is just doing its job, and maybe they think of it that way.

5

Horses are heavy, you can't pull them, even with a rope tied around their neck. What you have to do is chop into them and get your pieces, your horse steak, and just wrap it up in tinfoil right there. Hunks of horse in tinfoil. Which I'm glad I brought the tinfoil with me, because if not, then what? And I'm surprised at how many horse steaks you'll get out of a horse, when you use every part and I fill up Winifred's refrigerator and have enough for my refrigerator, even if I don't eat much meat myself. I haven't had anyone over to my apartment to look in my refrigerator because I don't want to have tinfoils full of horsemeat falling out and having to explain what they are. Doing what butchers do, butchering, is heavy too. The work, that is. Your arms get really tired after a while and so you need a break, and I'm pretty much over dealing in tinfoil and horse pieces all day, and there are quite a few flies around the horse, which horse I think is Hefner, but I can't tell because all horses look like horses. I just use one of the five names that Winifred's been using and vary them whenever I'm looking at a new horse. Of course, now I will only use four names to call the horses in the meadow who they are. They are who they are, and I think, why confuse myself with names, they all look like Winifreds to me anyway, and so now I call them Winifred, regardless of who they are, because horses don't really have names anyway. Really, it's just too much work to full-butcher the horse so I end up leaving it in the field. I'm not worried,

Winifred can feed herself. It was a worthwhile idea, but I'm not a butcher.

6

I rewatch the horse painter paint on the television show I recorded. The horse clutches the handle of the brush with confidence you know means the horse knows it's an artist. There is a dead horse in the middle of the field behind Winifred's witch house, out there with the four other Winifred horses, and I can still hear them, though only in my mind, whinnying and stomping about all jittery. And tinfoil. I call my friends to have me over for dinner, but they are busy, and they wonder why I didn't get back to them sooner: We had you for dinner over a week ago and we haven't heard from you since. Well, *Winifred*, I tell them, but I'm not sure if the answer is sufficient, or if they can parse the meaning: that one of Winifred's horses is dead out behind her house less a few tinfoils of horsemeat and plus some flies, but that's all, that's when I quit. For a couple of weeks after my friends are acting weird over the phone and I haven't been checking up on my good friend Winifred, I watch the video I recorded of the horse with a paintbrush clutched in its teeth. I re-watch it whenever I don't know what to do, and I don't leave my house, so I watch and watch, and I sit really close-up to the television to see if I can tell that the horse is actually an artist, or if it's all fake, what the horse is doing—just some dog trick. The horse seems serious though. Or at least I can't tell from how close I am to the television, and how close the horse is to the camera, whether or not the horse is faking it. The horse paints a canvas of blue lake over and over again and I don't think about Winifred—Hefner—or the other Winifreds out in the field behind Winifred's witch house. I don't think about Winifred proper, with her glasses, and her distaste for seeing things and operating like a normal person *my* age. She's older, so she has her excuses, she has a horse's name, but what else can be said of her? That she likes meat? Like that is enough to sustain a friendship? It gets arm-tiring being a pro bono butcher, and hot.

7

It's been a couple weeks, as I've said, and I think I can see it in the horse painter. I'm close enough to the television that it looks like the horse is the real thing, a real horse artist. I do some research and I decided to make amends with Winifred, for not getting her enough meat. And her horses, the four remaining Winifreds. I research making horse-talk and decide to teach them how to be artists themselves, and to make more of themselves than the food people will claim of them. I make it out to the house when the sun is out, so Winifred can see the blob of me that she sees, through her glasses. The grey house seems darker in the sunlight, I always think, and in Salem they would really love the way Winifred's house looked, to get their hysteria going. I bring the television with me and the recording of the horse painter, because I think Winifred might appreciate it, since she keeps horses. Through the windows, however, it seems that everything of Winifred's has been covered in linens. Like the furniture and other items are traditional ghosts, draped white, though without the eyeholes. I can see that it seems like Winifred might not be there anymore. I knock and knock on the windows and the door, but nothing happens. She must be lost, considering how Winifred can't see very well, and I imagine her walking around in one of the upper rooms of the house, walking into the ghost furniture on accident, knocking things over, because she has a problem with navigation. It doesn't matter, though. I'm figuring, even if we've been good friends, our friendship has become strained. Or, if not strained, I should move and give myself distance from horse-named women, whether or not that can be used as an excuse. As a result, I am out in the field behind Winfred's house, and the horses, who I've known well—they've always been there—are gone. I walk the field looking for Hefner—in death, now, I say his name—but he too is gone. It's easy to see they are gone, but I walk the field regardless, because you never know if you might find a paintbrush, or something else. It's not as important as it seems, but Winifred and I were good friends, though you should be careful with friends, if they have a horse's name, and keep horses, because there is something there, in how meat is consumed and what foods are artists, that has me wondering about going back to college and finishing up, maybe taking some horse-talking classes.

8

When I break into Winifred's abandoned house a week later than that, a man asks me, Excuse me there, ma'am, just what is it you think you're doing? The man wears hair on his face like he wants me to know that he's *that* kind of animal. I roll my eyes at him and say, Well, Winifred of course, hoping this amounts to an answer. He bristles, though. What do you know of our Winifred? I just walk on by, peeking under the linens at the couches and chairs, trying to find the ones that I thought might look good in my apartment. The man is following me and I don't look at him but it's obvious he has a look on his face like, *Just what do you think you're doing?*

I tell him, You look like her, you know, which is something
I assume, because he's probably her grandson. He says that
he looks nothing like her and why am I here, I don't belong
here, I need to get out. I walk up the stairs and he stays
standing in the entryway, arms folded. Get back down here,
he says, like he's the authority on where I should be. Right
when I've found the lamp I'm looking for, he's finally come
upstairs and he says, Now, this is my great grand-aunt's
house, you hear? I need you to leave here immediately or
I'll have the police escort you. I'm holding the lamp. I knew
you looked like her, didn't I? He tells me, no, he doesn't,
probably because Winifred is homely and has horse teeth.
He must know this. And give me that lamp! Later, when I've
subdued him and the police are on their way, we are sitting
on the porch and his name is Douglas. Douglas tells me that
Winifred is none of my concern now, and that for all intents
and purposes it's god that is the one to be having concerns.
I say to him, That's too bad, seeing as how she was so, and I
don't finish because I can't figure out what it is exactly. What
happened to the horses, I ask. What horses? Over there in
the field, my good friend Winifred had some horses. She
wasn't your friend, look at you. She was old and she didn't
know here from there, so just cut that shit right now. They
were Alpacas. I don't know what he means. And one of
them got one of those diseases where you run your head
into the bricks and Great Aunt Winifred, she was always
one to use every part of everything, never waste nothing,
and they think she took the animal and made meals out of
it and didn't cook the meals, or she didn't microwave them
long enough, and now she is where she is, and we all in
the family, well, we know where she is now. It's where she's
always been headed. Oh you bet, I say. After we fall in love

the police never arrive, but I tell Douglas that I had left the tape of the horse painter under Winifred's pillow up in her room and I tell him I'm not interested in a relationship right now, because it's just not good timing, but he doesn't seem bothered and isn't looking at me much, so I tell him I'm sorry to hear about the…he says alpacas and I say al-pac-as, and then I tell him that Winifred was a good friend of mine, I promise, and that maybe someday we should work on getting to heaven together, but he's already closed the door. Walking home, I think about what Winifred might be doing with that al-pac-a up in heaven and if that means anything for me as an artist, if I work hard enough, and I take the rest of the week to figure whether an al-pac-a can have a name like Madeline, Hefner, Bimmers, Cynthia, or Shondra—Winifred even.

SVEN

RE

ARRANGES

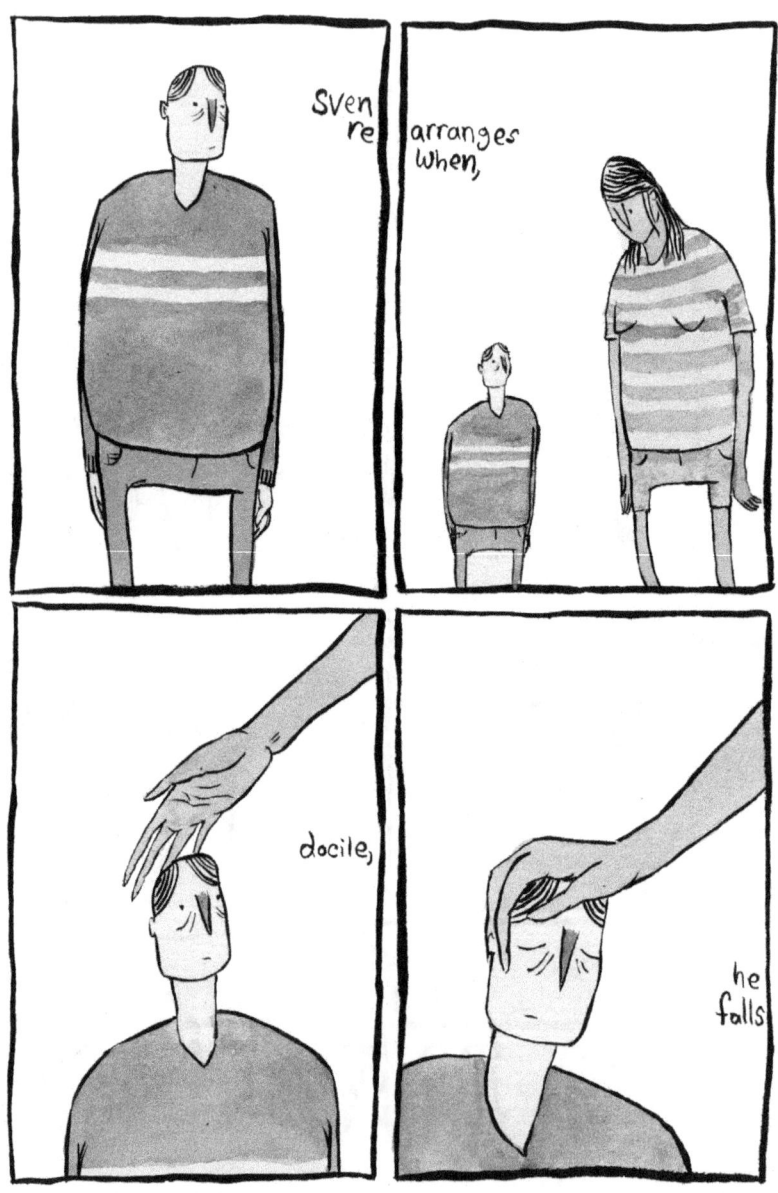

under Beth's palm-heat,

after

ward

expanding

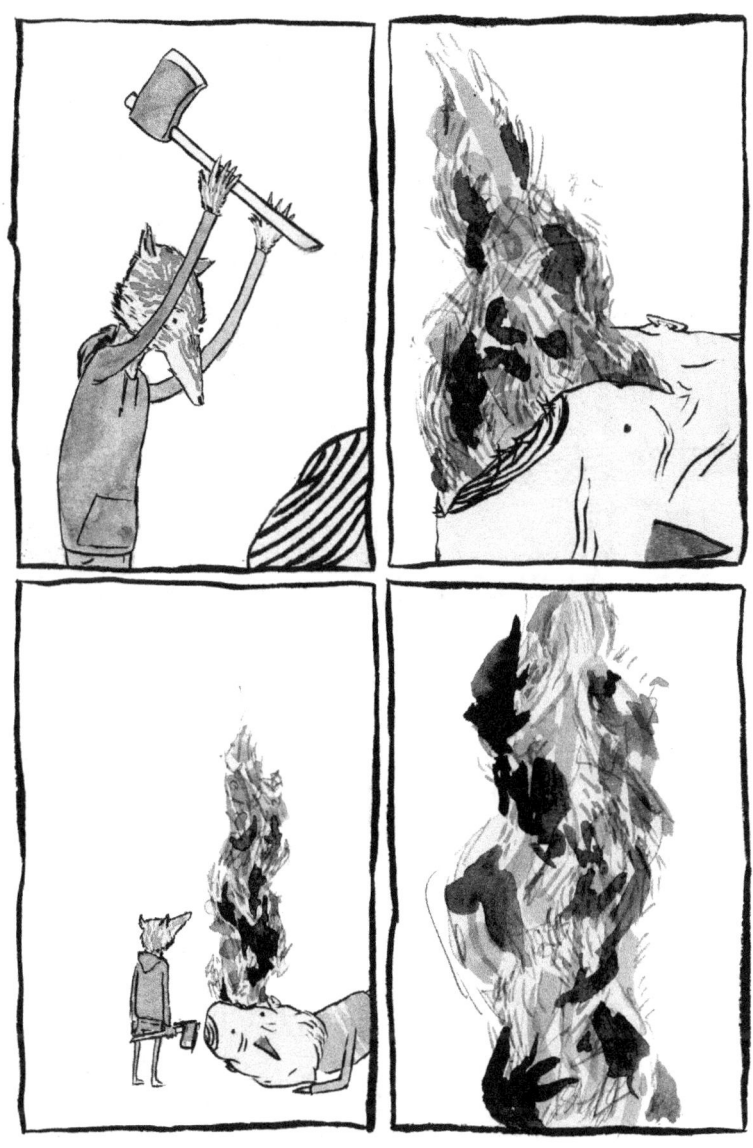

JOSH HENDERSON

IS ANNE BOLEYN

There was a queen situation earlier this week when Josh Henderson, devilishly, was Anne Boleyn—a regrettable decision in retrospect.

Did you say Anne Boleyn?

You heard what I said, Miranda.

Carole-Anne, he said—

Yeah, I heard him.

And then Lucy:

Who's Anne Boleyn?

They sat half-shaded, taking dignified sips of nothing from pink plastic teacups when he said it. Each paused a moment after the words were out, even Josh, weighing the significance and buoyancy of the words, spreading out the letters and then reattaching them. Carole-Anne, the oldest of the Henderson children, turned her head in her odd way, got up, and rushed inside.

The custom for the Henderson children, ever the sweet little demons, was to briefly educate themselves concerning what it was they were playing at. Something their parents encouraged, thinking to themselves (their parents), *what a terrific idea!* So, characters, historical or otherwise, fictional or not, whenever they fell out of their mouths, were quickly scooped up for examination. And thus, in the immediate aftermath of Joshua's declaration ("I *am* Anne Boleyn!"), small notes were taken as to what queenly thing was to proceed, procured from the bookshelf, from the family's edition of Encyclopedia Britannica (a healthy informer of the majority of their imaginary exploits).

It was a curious going-through-the-motions of imitation intelligence though—not that they were particularly unintelligent children, they were only moderately unintelligent—but they were lazy historians—Carole-Anne in particular—and Carole-Anne, having the responsibility for reading, due to seniority, ended up only half-reading the B Encyclopedia's *Anne Boleyn* entry, and with some apparent huffiness, producing small sighs as she skimmed.

She remained with the B volume for some time however, even after half-reading *Anne Boleyn*, though silently now, flipping through pages and gathering visual information from the pictures supporting certain entries: *baboon, barbwire, Barbie doll, black bear, bologna, burn.* According to Carole-Anne, the Britannica offered Josh—formally Joshua—three years of reign.

After deliberating the matter, the three Henderson sisters offered him three days and, he now a she and she, inexplicably, a queen, three miracles. It was a tidy equation: one day per historical year and three miracles per their esteem of queenliness. Anne, ever royally gracious, accepted:

Okay, so you got 3 days Josh, what more do you want?

It's Anne, Miranda; call me Anne or I'll put you in jail!

Your highness! Miranda's head lowly hovering, sarcastically, part of an extended curtsy.

I want full days though. Today's already half over!

Then you're still Josh until tomorrow.

It was good fortune for everyone that Carole-Anne was so authoritative in these types of situations.

Fine. Mom's making me do my stupid bath tonight anyways.

Groggily, Josh is halfway through a breakfast-time bowl of Count Chocula before he remembers, *I am Anne Boleyn!,* chocolate flecks in a waterfall from his mouth as she asserts her reign with tyrannical force.

You guys can't eat here! This breakfast table is for queens only!

Anne Boleyn, in a full dragon-pajama suit, standing unsteadily atop his stool, pointing at herself: *Queen!* Count Chocula shrapnel everywhere.

The younger two Henderson girls react, a knee-jerk response in their mouths, back-talking Joshua, but are cut, mid-retort, by Carole-Anne's sharp disapproving face and marvelous obedience to the queen herself, removing her cereal bowl (Cinnamon Life, now ashen with bits of chocolate and marshmallow) to the ground below the kitchen table. Miranda and Lucy, shocked, hesitantly follow suit, the three of them now—sisters—on the ground eating cereal, Josh grinning wildly and pouring a second bowl for Anne Boleyn.

• • •

It's Friday, but it's Good Friday, and the Henderson children are free from school. The young Hendersons are closely crowded in age, a tightly birthed quiver of children: four kids in five years, their mother opting to "get it over with," when planning the brood progeny with their father. Carole-Anne's status among them is further enhanced by her having advanced into junior high school, separated by two grade levels from the next oldest, Miranda, the latter three still towing the elementary line. It's forced Carole-Anne into something of a pseudo-mothering position. Still, there's a closeness among them, one that's affected a certain internal glomming, the children caught together by some sense of familial gravity, producing a sticky interdependence.

Noonish, sun-hot, the air melting into hazy ribbons, tyranny flourishes.

Get my royal goblet, ugly maids.

The Henderson girls, surprisingly, following Carole-Anne's example, are all too willing to serve their queen. The girls, bearing the sweat of a summery midday, maintain under the auspices of Josh, Anne Boleyning giddily; Carole-Anne inspiring Miranda, knowingly, and the two of them keeping Lucy, the youngest Henderson girl, in full tilt, not whining, as they shade Anne with leaves, fan her with leaves, stitch together a crown atop her head with twigs and leaves—his crew-cut head of infant-soft hair.

If you aren't wearing the crown, your highness, your royal abilities will be greatly diminished.

It's a spontaneous trap of Carole-Anne's since the twig-leaf halo has been woven with only enough strength for Josh to sit sedately in perfect posture, lest the crown, precariously perched, tumble away in the huff of an imperfect breath.

But I can't move with this thing on, it'll fall apart.

You're the one who chose to be the queen, Josh.

Anne! Call me Queen Anne or you have to go to jail! the outburst rustling her crown, causing shedding of a group of rear-sitting leaves. *See!?*

• • •

It's approaching dinnertime and Anne still hasn't performed her allotted daily miracle. All that's been produced in this queenly play is a haphazard crown (though, a crown, now, reinforced with additional leaves, twigs, grass, and various other yardly appendages, for greater structural integrity and greater queenly appearance, both). Queen Anne, smartly, decrees that the three allotted miracles need not occur in tandem with the three allotted years of rule: the three allotted days.

The Henderson parents are taking advantage of the weekend as well, as they often have, leaving Carole-Anne in charge: in charge of dinner, in charge of the dishes, and, if it comes down to it, in charge of bedtime.

Unsurprisingly, Carole-Anne's pseudo-motherhood carries on into the tooth-brushing and pajama-wearing of late evening, and, save for a few small queenly demands, Joshua settles himself under Carole-Anne's leadership, putting his Anne Boleyning aside, if only slightly. Once in bed, however, Joshua remains awake, thinking, considering his miracles and how he will plot his name into the encyclopedia books as a glorious queenly figure.

And the Henderson girls, sharing a room in accord with their parents' position on sleeping and genitalia, lay awake also, divulging, in cat-whispers, the secrets of unconditional maidliness, including imaginary missives, and, inspired by Carole-Anne, other, darker vagaries.

• • •

Saturday morning. It's set to be another scorcher, the weatherman said, holy as it is. The Henderson girls, by sheer willpower of their older-aged maturity (and by routine of their shared morning bus schedule), are up and at 'em, preparing an imperial breakfast for the still-slumbering (askewly at that) Queen Anne in her royal quarters (she having exhausted herself long into the night hours with thoughts of miracles).

Josh takes a moment to remember his role once awake, to be dainty, to accept the loveliness of buttered toast on her bedded lap, orange juice on the side table, Count Chocula (the cereal of queens) next to the orange juice.

That's good, that's right, Queen Anne confers.

We hope you like it, dear Your Highness.

Yes, Your Highness, we hope it is worthy of your splendid mouth.

A turn-faced giggle.

And your splendid fingers.

Of course. My chores now…

Josh is surprised, pleasantly, at how well his being Anne Boleyn is working out, the Henderson girls working heavily at his allotted chores, escorting him about the house on a royal pillow (though only a short number of trips before reason gives way, Joshua being a well proportioned boy). And he's never been considered in so splendid a manner before, particularly his fingers.

In the midday heat, ribbons of air yet again, Queen Anne demands renovation of the castle she inhabited the previous day: sandbox towers, a poorly dug moat. The Henderson maids oblige by stacking nearby branches and debris into the sandpit, their actual home bordering the actual woods, for purposes of walling up Queen Anne's imperial fortress.

• • •

It's near the ending of the construction that Queen Anne produces her first miracle, quite possibly by accident, Josh is uncertain, a bit startled by his own queenly display, as, properly crowned (a crown growing more elaborate by the hour), Josh's hair—Queen Anne's hair—crew-cut and infant-soft, lengthens by an inch.

The brief swell of hair is so short as to be inconsequential, and even Lucy, busily building up the nesting structure crowning Queen Anne's head, takes the difference in length as a fallacy propagated by her blinking.

This, however, proves to be incorrect, and measurably so, when, after another moment, the familiarly crew-cutted infant-softness extends itself, abruptly—*My goodness!*—from the nape of Joshua's neck deep into the geography of his middle-back. It's an amiable spurt of growth that pushes sections of the crown into disarray.

Carole-Anne? Lucy defers, and Carole-Anne, arms filled with sticks, looks on it expectantly, smiling—satisfying both Lucy and Miranda.

In seeing the pleased looks upon his sister's faces, Josh resumes her previous dictatorial air, demanding that one of the Henderson girls shade her again, Carole-Anne quickly accepting the change in task, today using an umbrella to shade Queen Anne and herself, as the two younger sisters toil sweatily with the building of Queen Anne's royal fortress.

• • •

By mid-afternoon it's finished.

Queen Anne, a lemonade in hand, shaded, fanned, a bed of royal pillows atop the coarse sandbox sand, and the sweaty smell of sand all over every part of each of them.

The evening offers a cooled respite, softening also Queen Anne's demands upon the Henderson sisters. Loosening their collars, their leashes, allowing them to become congenial with the queen, to speak freely, to sit among the pillows, the tiny fortress now containing the four of them, Queen Anne and her maidens, all puzzled together and laughing, consuming treats from the royal eatery, the remaining contents of the Cinnamon Life cereal box, sand and sugar crunching between their teeth.

• • •

The Hendersons gathering together for their Sunday morning routine: *Easter morning!*, their parents remind them, *Carole-Anne, can you make sure everyone gets ready?* The Henderson girls dressing in their best dresses, Josh putting on his Sunday slacks, clipping a tie to the collar of his white shirt with a browning stain around the neck and wrinkles up and down the sleeves and back because it's been crumpled up all week in the corner of his bedroom.

Joshua does not cut her hair.

Queen Anne, what are you wearing?

What? What do you mean, it's Sunday—

But you are the queen, and it's Easter—wait right here, I'll find you something better.

Carole-Anne emerges from her room with her favorite old Eastertime dress, a silvery-blue getup with a giant purple bow hanging from the back, just above the hips, and pompous frills descending from the shoulders.

I'm too big for it now, but I've never let anyone else wear it (the Henderson family wardrobe was prone to constantly being handed down)*, seems only fitting that you be the first, on this your last queenly day.*

———

Carole-Anne dresses the dress over Anne quickly, right over the top of his already-readiness, her long hair remaining tucked beneath the collar of the dress in the aftermath. Their mother calls upstairs: *Joshua, girls! It's time to get going!*

The Henderson parents don't notice having four girls on this particular Sunday, only noticing a much smoother routine in getting the children ready and into the Astro van, each thinking to themselves (their parents), *what a wonderful job we are doing, raising these children.* The girls let Josh sit next to the window, whisper nice things to him. They're halfway to church before he considers, even in the rush of his being quite literally *dressed* by Carole-Anne, his royal calling. Queen Anne is no longer the dictatorial tyrant she had exhibited in herself earlier. Complementing and appreciating her subjects, allowing them to leave to the bathroom and for drinks from the drinking fountain during sermon.

The girls offer prayers on behalf of Queen Anne. During sermon, notes are passed to Josh detailing the diverse talents each girl is willing to offer him. Instead of excluding him, they allow him to participate in their sermon-time games: tic-tac-toe, connect the dots, drawing pictures of animals—quiet activities from which Josh is normally excluded. He leans forward and they scratch his back with their augmented fingernails.

In the service of his subjects, Josh and the Henderson girls are unsurprised when the second miracle afforded him is produced. Though, the congregation ascribes it mostly to Jesus and some to the devil:

Amidst the closing prayer of the service you could see the bird, tight and lumpen in Josh's throat, as it muscled upward into his mouth, filling his cheeks, and then, once his lips parted, its beak, then its head, peeking out into the air, looking both ways in that dart-quick way of small birds, as if at a crosswalk, before pushing his teeth wide and fluttering into the wide-open chapel air—and startled screams erupted from the congregation.

• • •

Sunday evening is getting ready for school on Monday: packing backpacks, organizing homework—it's been a long weekend. Queen Anne crowned, demanding the girls' Easter-night desserts. Miranda is unwilling until Carole-Anne cuts her with a look. Queen Anne is gracious though, patiently waiting for Miranda to come to terms, to turn over her banana-mushed ice cream sundae.

You still've got one more miracle, you know, Carole-Anne floated—*Queen Anne,* the name lifting up and hanging over the kitchen table.

Hey, why don't we go over to the elementary playground tonight? You can finish out ruling over us there, said Miranda.

Anne Boleyn, shoveling in shovels full of ice cream—that extra ice cream afforded to royalty—mostly avoiding the bananas, absorbing the suggestions from her royal maids.

Sure.

• • •

The school, Featherstone Elementary School, is not so far away. Only a couple blocks of housing and a stretch of field. A potato chip factory stands across the street from the school, pumping salty oils into the air. It's closed on weekends, but the burnt potato chip smell is still there, is always there, churning oily salts into the lungs and bloodstreams of the attendant schoolchildren and faculty.

It's a late arrival for the Henderson children, later than they're usually out: the moon beginning to show while the sky hangs on to as much of its sun-brightened skirt as possible. The night, though, inevitably rising or falling or consuming.

I'm going down the slide! Joshua screams; Lucy, the closest of the sisters to Joshua's age, running along behind him to join.

Carole-Anne unpacks a coil of rope. Girls, as we know—sisters in particular—will see a queen situation through to its proper end.

There is an oddness to the turning air, something Miranda begins only partially to recognize in her older sister, Miranda being the most clued-in to the queen-happening that's preparing to happen. Carole-Anne, having prepared for it all along, has long sat in the odd air and is plenty accustomed, by now, to its vibrations; Lucy is still a bit young, despite having heard, having listened in on the late night sister-talk, about what it is to end an Anne Boleyning.

Josh and Lucy have descended the slide numerous times by the time Carole-Anne and Miranda approach, join them.

What's the rope fo—Miranda smacking Lucy over the head in her absentmindedness.

Ow!

Yeah, what is the rope for?

Well, Your Highness, this is something akin to a necklace—you'll notice the loop—something to test your royal stature, as it were. Your final miracle, oh Anne, I think will have something to do with wearing yourself through this.

The odd casualness in Carole-Anne's voice—fitting the odd air—registers everything clearly in Lucy now.

The girls, all four of them, standing atop the slide, their hair blowing limply upwards in a brief rush of summer breeziness.

Queen Anne stood steadily as Carole-Anne wrapped her neck in rope when, just as she'd fixed her knot—meant to slide, or "slip," as the title of the knot inferred, having a well illustrated and easily imitated instructional image to coincide with the article found in the family's Britannica's

K volume—Lucy sitting down, crossed-legged, humming
to herself nervously, Miranda looking hopefully for an
accidental mis-knotting within the knot-work of Carole-
Anne, something that might collapse the formation of rope
rather than the loop of rope around Queen Anne's neck,
and Carole-Anne, tying the tail-end coil to the safety barring
surrounding the platform, telling Queen Anne, *okay, stand
here,* and Joshua readily, aloofly complying.

WELL-WISHING THE WEIGHT OF
SOMETHING KEVINLY PIECEMEAL

(daughters, hammers)

Wearing a suit and hat, an unnamed man (sleuth) waits, expects a small woman and a hammer. It's nighttime in an area where small-woman traffic is high and it doesn't take long before there she is. Underarm, there's the neck, vesicles, vessel-wiring, links of bone: the body's wide open and she drags it hastily. He follows. Finds now there's two women, back in the shed examining and hammering, examining and hammering. Filling the body with a bucket of nails, rods, and bolts. He uses an indoor voice. Says, *Nice weather out.* Says, *Missing a few parts there, are we?* No verbal response, no physical response, just two small women hammering, hammering. He observes silently. Not looking up, one of them upstarts abruptly: *Mom!?* and he says, *Okay, okay,* and excuses himself.

(a good wife will pick horse)

Several stern Kevins won't amount to the Kevin they're hammering, tongued senseless, and less a good portion of what it is people have and are alive with. Operating on a sleuthing register, the suit-wearing man returns, takes notice of the hinge-parts: elbows, wrists, knees, ankles, etcetera, through the doorway. And the mandibles, opened and toothy: Kevin. It's a positive ID. He excuses himself to find Betty: small woman with a hammer—she's in charge. When Betty says, *Look, cattle work just fine, and we have plenty—all we need,* he says, *Though, have you considered horse?* When she says nothing, he says, *Think about the properties of a horse,* winks, and tips his hat.

(smalltown heat / hype)

—*Summery, hot like hell out here—kitchen weather, to be certain— and only two days 'til our yearend rigmarole. Tony, what do you think about Okkerstown's chances?*

—*You've got the hot part right. You know, I got up and out of bed this morning and the durned swampcooler's cracked! Can you picture me and Frisbee, head-to-toe in sweat?*

—*Poor dog.*

—*Anyways, you got to make sure them boys get hydrated, is the point. Okkertown's got a good shot, they keep water in their bellies.*

—*Right you are, Tony. Though, well-hydrated or not, they still have to deal with #23, Billy Wiggins. Now, have you seen an arm like this before? I feel like I'm watching a, a...*

—*Oh, there's no stopping Billy Wiggins, he's a phenom. And Okkerstown's got to be scrambling after their defensive coordinator, Kevin Briarly, was caught in the middle of that Al Queeda deal happened yesterday at the Center Street Albertsons...*

—*That's right. And to the Briarlys, from everyone here at OSL1600 and our affiliates, our prayers are with you.*

(kevin)

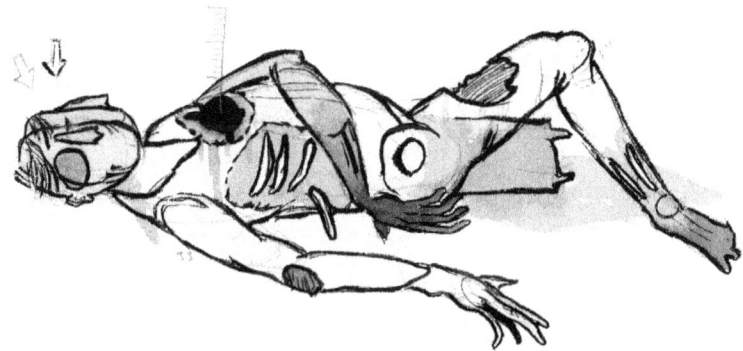

(alignments, audibles, ands)

When handling the meantime, the unnamed man reviews scouting tapes at the close-by motel, watching for sideline abnormalities, hiccups, memorizing hand signals and their corresponding field alignments. He revitalizes his suit at the drycleaner. Some hours, then back in proximity of the women, dwarfish, all of them with hammers: constructing back that first of Kevins, praying: *May he reconfigure the starting roster of the high school football team.* Small women with an interest in prep sports. Defense, particularly. Sisters. (And with hammers.) Traveling daily: in the mornings to the shed, in the evenings from. The man with his hat stands up against the street lamp across the street waiting for their mother. Betty moseys out casually (as expected): *About horse... Because we seem to be dry of cattle...*That and, well, and and and. The streetlamp man is uncomfortable, excludes himself from participating in Betty's advances. Departs.

(apple-water revival)

It's when Betty tilts her head, lets her hair out of its bun it's been bundled in, hair sliding down her neck, against her shoulder, that Kevin—an apple dead in his mouth— looks neckward (horse eyes), and, thinking about how, once he'd toothed through the skin, chewing up that neck is going to be a fair bit of work, apple-water on his tongue, running down his chin—*He's awake!*, the youngest says. Gathering herself, *He's awake.* The way anyone scrambles anymore (quarterback) these girls are scrambling. Tools for stabilizing. Time. He's swallowed the cheek of apple he'd been turning over in his mouth, but he continues chewing his teeth together, masticating emptily. Sound like tiny creaking floorboards, his teeth-cheeks rubbing together. Nuzzling porcelain dolls. The unnamed man (sleuth) is crouched, listening in through the shed walls. Finds a loose knot in the wood and peeks through. Kevin is staring at her neck, he notices she notices, apple fluid glistening off his chin. Betty: *Kevin, you're grinding. Kevin!* Kevin: Kevin: *Oh. My goodness, oh...I'm sorry.*

(verbal strides / cutting)

—*What I don't understand is, if they're running the forty-two option, why not tell Jensen to keep it.*
—*Every time?*
—*Every time, because regardless of whether the defensive end bites down on him, Jensen's a warhog, he'll tunnel in for three or four yards every time.*
—*You have a point, Tony, though I'm going to have to stop you right there so that we can provide a moment for our sponsors, for whom we are very grateful. I'm here with Tony Mackelroy for our weeklong lead up to the State Championships, contended by our very own Okkerstown Tigers who'll be facing off against the undefeated Minderville Pooch Hounds. We've been discussing the forty-two option and Okkerstown's freshman marvel: quarterback, Kip Jensen. After these messages we'll return with an update on defensive coordinator Kevin Briarly's status, live from Okkerstown Hospital—after these messages.*

(fixtures of patriarchal hand-wetting)

You can, Betty discovers, add an inch of circumference to Kevin's head by placing an imaginary item, variable in size, inside Kevin's mouth, then working out the headspace with a hammer (inserted through the area gaping at the crown). Because the hammer is a complex mathematical device, Betty does not worry about the corrugations wrinkling through Kevin's hair—they will not do damage to what imagination is holding still in Kevin's mouth. And the hammer will calculate any small differences, automatically adjusting for anomalies and so forth. Do, though, consider wearing gloves, as Betty finds out the hard way.

(kevin)

(sifting up the holes, cleaning: almost)

It's when Betty takes the unruffled portions of Kevin, that capillary mass—what hasn't dissolved—and imbues it with energy, that the vacuum begins.

(every third down)

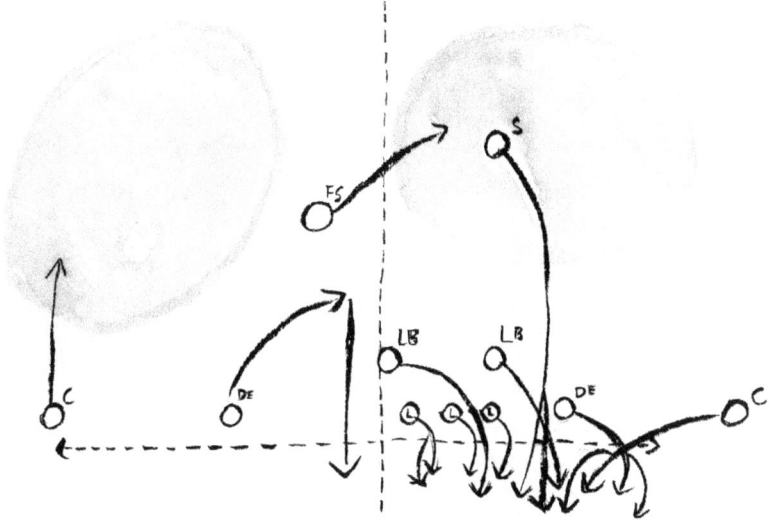

(brick version)

It's agreed that the stomach be filled with bricks collected from under the bleachers. A strong digestive option. An altogether agreed upon component of what Kevin should be (Kevin). The unnamed man, well-suited, sneaks into the shed and peeks over their shoulders while they're tipping the wheelbarrow of it all in, hoping to get in a word or two amidst the rumble. It's loud. He slips under the girls' arms as they're hefting, getting good and tight to Kevin's open ear, saying, *Kevin, think about the deep game. Think about post routes and fly routes and let them have whatever they can run for. Think about your safetys and your cornerbacks. Let 'em give cushion. You'll need to hold onto the deep parts of the field for dear life.* A daughter takes notice, Betty too: sees, hears. The man tips his hat, says *Good day* and departs.

(summer endtimes)

—And in what figures to be the story of this match-up, Kevin Briarly's been slated to return to the Okkerstown sidelines as the Tigers' defensive coordinator.

—It really is a miraculous recovery, isn't it Tim? From what I've heard, they pulled ten-odd pounds of Al Queeda shrapnel out of him. Can you believe it? Ten pounds!

—An absolute miracle. And the report we're getting is he's not able to walk yet, but they plan to have him out there in his hospital bed. One of those contraptions with a motorized back piece so they can sit him up and keep some IVs in him and whatnot.

—And thank heavens for it. When you consider the marvels of modern medicine with relation to this story, it's just, it's...Kevin Briarly would not have wanted to miss this game! Especially over some Al Queeda scuffle, I'll tell you that much.

—He's certainly a patriot. And beyond that, word is he's enacting some major changes to Okkerstown's defensive strategy.

—That's right. This whole deal may end up being more a blessing than a tragedy.

(betty, righteousness)

The unnamed man (sleuth) is out of his element, is in love with Betty. He is not alone. Men compacted into truck beds have been arriving for days, have been making positions to woo in the absence of Kevinly hearsay, Kevinly leg strength. What defense there's been: daughters with hammer loops sewn into their dresses, holstering what tools they're meant to, at either end of the porch, batting eyes—smokescreen—

and a well-oiled backdoor. It's inappropriate. He decides not to patrol the backdoor. He decides not to enter the kitchen bearing flowers and cattle. He decides not to place lips near the neck or wrist or ankle of anything resembling anything named Betty, not to press forward, or be pulled, up the stairs, into the bedroom, shirt Betty-tugged along. It never ends well with Betty. But it always ends.

(with unspended time)

In terms of wellbeing, Kevin isn't out of the woods. Though, the workable horse parts, cattle, and the remnants of brick and mortar are, it is assumed, working. He is and has his eyes open. (Horse.) They will give him to himself for an hour before game time: dark wooden shack. From there, it'll be their hands and a method of pushing familiar to hospitals. This is the nameless man's final opportunity. He takes notice of Kevin. For Kevin, things are operating chromatically. The unnamed man (sleuth) knows this, carries a wide brush. Paints everything shut while whispering, *Always rush on third downs, always rush on third downs.* When he hears the backdoor of the house—Betty wondering after the sleuth, why he's not in with her while Kevin gears up for the game—he wipes the dust off his shirt and turns the brush against himself, disappearing into the corner of the room. He has performed admirably. He will be rewarded.

(kevin)

(proper pissing, postgame)

—*You have to give credit where credit's due. The Pooch Hounds put together a marvelous season, and tonight's game was no exception, defeating the Okkerstown Tigers 73 to 3.*

—*As much as I hate to say it, Joe: you're right. The Pooch Hounds played amazingly, and Billy Wiggins in particular. I mean, 448 yards passing! 156 yards rushing! Okkersville's lucky to have shared the field with a player like Wiggins. And that's something they will be able to take away from this game, something they'll always remember: having shared the field with Billy Wiggins.*

—*Wiggins was phenomenal, there's no doubt about that. And with a performance like this, the stadium half-filled with recruiters, we are going to see a lot more of these Pooch Hound kids in top-grade schools at the collegiate level.*

—*Oh, there's no doubt. I mean Bridger, Callfield, Mendenson, Rogers, not to mention Wiggins, these schools will be throwing every pony they have at these kids.*

—*It's true. One only hopes that they can take advantage of the opportunity and tuck a nice education under their belts while they're at it.*

—*Joe, I've always been fervent supporter of education.*

(requiem song)

SUBMERGE/ASCEND

Down there against the shore of the river, tearfully, letting it all into the run of water from out our eyes, it's unclear: have we ingested it properly? Now we think yes, now we think no. Having money is a difficult thing not to have. There's consolation-making, and hands make hands on backs, how we make due with what we've made, after having been pouring away down there: on the banks. We walk back up. Running low on window washer fluid so our heads are in there, sideways, beneath the hood of the truck. We'll overfill the canister with tear-water and so the rest of it's left for the dirt, help the drought. It's hours, nearly. Fix our shirtsleeves, get into the truck—shoulder to shoulder to shoulder— engine hacking up idly. You get to the point you spread it out flat enough you're inhaling it. And we've cried enough. Though, even we are, we think, oblivious to the level at which the idea has entered into and integrated with our body and blood cells. Bearing a certain amount of sweat on our faces. And the river, risen, insignificantly perhaps to the casually passing passerby, but not at all insignificant to the river (if you know anything about rivers). (We have river-understanding.) And so we're driving towards downtown, roll the windows low so that the wind'll get the slick off our faces and have a look at one another once we've parked so we know everything's ordered, before we get out and get at it. Everything. It's a river truck, anyone can see that, so there's some sense of where getting into the truck bed will get you. We dress for it. Polite, homely, wrinkled, standing in front of the truck downtown, and, yes, yes, that's where we're intending on going, would you like coming with us, it's a fine drive, not as long as you'd think, and you'd be surprised how getting some wind into your ears will clear you. And there's more, we mention, in succession, stumbling over each other, with talk, but sincerely (a soft charm). A small handful of city people, an invisible fraction, ones that have been beaten by the city longest; the ones that, even when they were children and only viewed it through the television, the city weighed in on them, leaned onto their houses, sucked the blood out of their heads. So they get in, wingtip shoes, suit coats off and held underarm, heels, pulling the ribbons out of their hair. A handful. We smile at them as we'd planned to. Still, only a few of them tangle together, leg over leg, in the truck bed. It's some amount of courage, getting out of the city at noontime, or anytime, in the open bed of a river truck, us three sardining up front in the cab. But getting wind in your ears is, they agree, silently, what it is we said it was. And the drive ends, before it grows too long. We said that too. The river. We handle them kindly, the city-weary, assisting each out of the truck bed one by one. And leading the group down to the river, through the brush and high bramble. Let the dirt feel you, we don't have any money, can't wash your clothes or skin, but it's its own reward, you can trust us. And they do. Or they're tired. One or the other. We're happy with them and they'll be happy with us. Weariness will work more heavily than a lot of things, we've come to understand. It is the determination of whatever is ingestible. Uncontested. That feeling, grumbling raw at the core. And they'll get what it is that will revive them. It's handy that we're available to give it to them, they think. Part of the shine of the idea is that you can accomplish it without any funds, but oh, how making money would make making it make more sense. We'd imagined, naively, added so much pomp in the beginning. Adorning the river and its shores with color-matching bric-a-brac. Burning fires. Reality ended us in an understanding of bare bones-ing it, as we have; as it is. We lead them into the river and we're happy to find ourselves waist deep in the center. All of our shoes and theirs, those city-wearied saints, are lined up back at the bank. We all watch each other and we close our eyes and it's not long before they submerge us in the slow current of the river and we can only flail underwater, not because we mean to give them a hard time, but because our bodies have been given instructions outside of ourselves to do that when being put under with city-wearied hands. It's a dirt-filled river and opening our eyes reveals not much. It's amazing giving in. Having white shirtsleeves and slender typing wrists holding us under until it is we are heading upward eternally, escalating, tenderly attending to each other as dogs in winter at night. And then black.

ARTO'S HEADSPACE

PAUL'S TOMB: A TRIUMPH?

This happens: Cleveland and the troops unwittingly find a tomb. Paul's tomb. Paul isn't an uncommon name; maybe Cleveland, maybe one of Cleveland's troops, knew Paul. Or read about Paul. Regardless: a resurrection takes place. One of the wetter resurrections of the past few decades, facts be facts (Cleveland and the boys using plenty of liquids when they resurrect). Buckets of water suspended above some spiraling wooden gears, a pulley or two—two pulleys—and Paul's caving frame fenced in by the wetbrown equipment—lucky they had their equipment!—everything soaked and pulsing, rigidly. There's a steady, high-pitched creaking (resurrection is a noisy enterprise) and then a happening: Paul up and standing forth, wiping the sweat of resurrection from his brow. Cleveland and the gang exchange toiled grins, exhausted, but satisfied at their success. Some spit exits their mouths, marries the dirt. He, Paul, wobbles forward, bracing himself on the frame of the tomb door. Centuries have thinned him to a tight sack of leathery bones. His hair, his fingernails, now long, patchy threads of deadened protein. A ruffled portion over his ear. The right one, from Cleveland's position. It's not the sight one expects to see. Cleveland, too, thinks so: resurrection isn't what he thought it would be. (Where was the silken aura? The spectral illumination? The confetti?) Have they performed it properly? Perhaps not. It's a smaller triumph than originally expected. And now what?

The resurrected Paul, noticing the quizzical looks of Cleveland and his cronies, the questioningness sharp on their faces, makes a suggestion: I think if I had a towel to dry off, I might look a pinch more comely, do you agree?

Kendall is positioned near the back of the group. Kendall doesn't mind saying so: I'm bored. I say we just get rid of it. Let's get rid of the head, and all of it really.

Paul contends through a dry, wispy, cloth-spewing exhale: Perhaps, he pauses, finger up in the air, pausing. Perhaps, I could stay a while. I just arrived, didn't I? I could massage your feet, each one of you—and stir up some tea while you each manage some sitting time? I imagine there are plenty of activities we could think up with some of this daylight.

They, the group of them, exchange looks, bemused, having locked jaws. Cleveland says, Well Paul, you see, we're not much for foot massages, particularly when performed by meatless palms. And you have meatless palms. Also, tea is not our sport. Not in the least. We're *men*.

Ah, well, Paul continues, perhaps we could attend to a lake somewhere—are there any lakes near here?—up a good tire swing. I could read to you all as you wade about in the water. I don't know what books you have on you, but I'm a handsome sight-reader.

Now Paul, Cleveland responds, what's this of reading? What do you make of us? Students? We are the type to resurrect—*re-sur-rect*—not to wet our hair in a lake or float belly-up like some lazies. You're pitching us tire swings? Our status is this: MEN [Cleveland holding up a black painted sign with "MEN" written in capital letters].

Then, quickly—no thinking here—it happens with shovels. Lots of smashing and cleanly shattered marrow. Little blood. The whole lot of them converging upon him as one. And so it is that the new Paul is collapsed upon by a heap of shovels, all thunderous and clanging, the light particles of old skin lifting from the ruckus, then floating softly back down to the earth.

· · ·

Instead: The "MEN" think on it and, following Cleveland's lead, pull out retractable chairs, opening them to their furthest, on their stretchedest joint, their shovels unsullied and free from guilt. It's a few minutes of rustling, but eventually, after settling their chairs, they sit deep, pondering. The possibilities! We did go to the effort of resurrecting him, they think. In the ponderous silence an opportunity for kissing sneaks up. An opportunity for kissing? Such moments are hard to define, but, inexplicably, they occur, and—as it is at this moment—often when one least expects. Paul acts oblivious, leaning back casually against the outer wall of the tomb, dryly whistling (he's never learned whistling). The cloud of opportunity weighs uncomfortably on the "MEN," hovering low, pecking at them. Its eventual departure is a relief to all.

Paul takes advantage of the opportunity-cavity left by the opportunity-for-kissing. I don't mean, spoken sheepishly, to burden your ponderings, but (and we imagine that Paul's revived heart is thumping with anticipatory madness here), but, what are the chances that lemonade or a lemon-fizz drink is available? I'm parched. I prefer the pink kind, but yellow's okay by me.

Immediately, Paul has a glass in his hand, a chair to sit in, an umbrella for shade. It appears that Cleveland's men can be very accommodating. Perhaps they're not so ravenous.

Someone speaks up. It's Dallin. Lanky Dallin.

You know, when we were making our way up here there was those train tracks we passed. We could try him out on those.

It's a couple hours before the train—just a teenage train, a lemon-fizz train happily enough, fizz drinks steadily tumbling from the back of the caboose—is turning the corner, Paul's left arm stretched across the track, not willingly of course, but strictly tied now and unmoving, Cleveland and his crew, a half-moon audience all straddling their 10-speeds, the bicycles dirty from the trip (Paul riding handlebars with Cleveland), a few of them wearing earphones, dubstep pulsing, R&B, the train trolleying closer and closer, cringing in advance of Paul, that metal chugga chugga burning against the tracks, but it's too loud, and, after some minutes or so, minutes spent mulching through flesh and marrow, the train is gone, and Paul lying there, still, his arm segmented at the wrist and at the shoulder, releasing him from the track.

Paul's blood, archaic as it was, coagulated into thin strings that hooped limply, hanging long from his opened arm.

Now what?

• • •

Now This: One arm gone, Paul gets grumpy. Ill-tempered arm-folding requires two arms. Still, Paul manages to adequately convey his grumpiness. Don't be like that Paul. How about if you make the next pick? Cleveland's offer doesn't change any of the details on Paul's grumpy face. Cleveland and his company are embarrassed. Eventually, Paul does accept Cleveland's offer:

I'd like to change my name.

They gasp. Marv, a taller member of Cleveland's crew, falls from his bike. Fortunately for Marv, parked near the back, few notice.

Call me Bruce.

Hesitation abounds. This is a big change for Cleveland and the guys. They resurrected a Paul, not a Bruce. But, in the end, Cleveland submits:

Alright, Bruce.

Paul, now Bruce, immediately grows a full handlebarred mustache, thick and black, knife-sharp at the tips. The implications of being named Bruce are marvelous. The men provide Bruce with sunglasses, neon, triangles running along the arms. They are *very* accommodating.

To the beach! Bruce proclaims, his lone arm outstretched. Excited, the men begin to foot at their pedals. Cleveland, however, is not so excited as his crew. Why is this Bruce character suddenly so cool? he thinks. *I'm* cool. Perhaps Cleveland is a tad insecure because he himself has never been able to develop a full face of hair. Instead, for Cleveland, it grows in all patchy, his rough cheeks barren but for a few tangled strands of beard. He likewise has found he is unable to cultivate any visible growth of mustache on his upper lip, his red-blonde hair appearing mostly transparent, even when conditioned for shine in the daylight. The inability to grow facial hair weighs heavily on his status as a leader of "MEN." But he says nothing.

Riding now the stretch toward the shore, Bruce perched on Cleveland's handlebars, not unlike a prince, Cleveland green with envy, his nose cartoonish, angrily red, the handlebars of Bruce's mustache fluttering against the breeze, the handlebars of Cleveland's bike trembling lightly, pleasantly, expectedly, Bruce doe-eyed at the prospect of a beachside suntan, Cleveland with an idea: the brakes.

The Brakes!

Bruce unprepared. Bruce soaring. Bruce tumbling and crashing. The men stopped amidst the commotion, astonished. Bruce, a contorted heap. Cleveland off his bike, approaching calmly, seemingly, grips Bruce by the skin, still wet and loose from the exertion of resurrection, and shakes out his bones. It's enough to end him; again.

• • •

Instead, back to this:

Instead of that, this:

• • •

This happens: Paul resurrects, a tormenting figure, ragged and uncertain-of-step, his sick, yellow eyes lounging low in their sockets. Cleveland and the troops are not impressed, disgusted actually.

Seriously, Cleveland, why'd we do this?

Shut it, Kendall. Let me think.

And they pause while he thinks.

Got any ideas boss? says Dallin. Lanky Dallin.

Nope, can't think of any. Let's get real: we're not "MEN." We might as well ask our mothers.

By this time Paul has gone wandering, in a slow, lumbering shuffle a hundred or so feet away, silent, simply wandering, like a lost Alzheimer patient. Cleveland has a couple of the men herd him back toward the group, then telephones a busing service in order to travel their mothers into camp.

It was some hours before they arrived, hours in which the yo-yo made a brief appearance, infiltrating the minds and knotting the fingers of various members of the troop, lovingly enchanting them until Cleveland, the taskmaster, restored the manly demeanor (a demeanor one expects of individuals or groups performing resurrection) with a reminder—a silent reminder—enacted simply by his flashing a black painted sign with "MEN" written in capital letters, and the yo-yos were pocketed. It was a span of hours in which the resurrected Paul was lost wandering no less than three times, and was eventually tied by the ankle to a shovel which was operating now as an anchor, having been submerged deeply into the soil; hours in which the closing of eyes was common and not considered an admission of weakness, as it previously had been, there being so many hours that passed before they, their mothers, arrived.

The bus arrives. It is heavyset with the musk of womenry. Their mothers exit the bus, nostril's humming, engulfed in an astral float of dust—their own particle history—orbiting them constantly. It's been some years since they'd bused their mothers in on a job. Cleveland picking at his throat like a harp, noting their birdlike hunches, the course of wrinkles rivering their skin, their matted spheres of translucent hair, their spectacles, their dresses shingled thickly in black oil paints, their heads hanging forward as if supported by nooses. They've finally exited in full, the tallest one's mouth warbling, motheringly doling out wavered condemnations with a measured smile.

The group is, for the most part, too far out of range to hear.

Paul takes some initiative, does some politicking, the dumb bag of bones, and introduces himself to the whole line of them, shaking the hand of each, his cold fleshy grip slippery like a descaled fish, freshly blooded, matching the ancient women bone for bone in each transaction. After allowing their pleasantries, their little introduction, Cleveland lays it out on the table: We've resurrected him, now what?

They huddle, briefly, though, the time it takes for them to gather together into a huddling and then return to their original formation, a strict line, a wall of motherhood, is not quick. The taller one, previously noted for mouthing wavered condemnations, is provided with a bullhorn by Marv (she being his mother specifically): He was gentle with us, handling our wrists and fingers. He seems harmless, sonlike. He seems to be as unhealthy as any of you have been at any point and to have the possibility for being as purposeless as each of you have turned out to be, to have a knack, possibly, as each of you have had, at one point or another, for the piano, though we expect, as was the case with you, each one of you, that he would, after a lengthy period, right when he would begin to catch his stride—the stride-catching period being after a year, maybe two years—would bear down on us, whining about how he didn't want to play the piano anymore. And we, being mothers, would refuse him for as long as we could, but we are mothers after all, not devils, not sons, and so, of course, as we did with each one of you, each and every one, we would submit, eventually, allow him to quit, to quit playing the piano, even after we told him how much he would regret it, and even after we said he would regret it, he would quit, just like each one of you quit, just as you were catching your strides, and now, how do you feel now? Ashamed? Filled with regret? (They did, they felt ashamed and filled with regret, all of them wanted to be able to play the piano, to tear through some ragtime number at a moment's notice, for a ragtime girl, for their mothers.) And, this being the case, us considering him as a son, not unlike one of you, we, therefore, we consider him dead. We suggest a shallow pond.

To this, Cleveland takes Paul and immediately drops his head down off his shoulders (Paul's head off Paul's shoulders), plip plop, just like that. Then, of course, for the sake of Marv's mother's suggestion, plants Paul's everything-from-the-shoulders-down portion in a nearby pond of sufficient shallowness.

Wait is he…?

Nope. No sir. He is not.

• • •

Actually, though: Paul never resurrects. Not ever. The men
all sullen—heads down, shoulders up, like impoverished
vultures. A few begin weeping and, subsequently, end up
being taken in the arms of others, less shaken, for a rarely
had physical-type comfort. Cleveland, overtired from
his resurrecterly exertions, packs Paul up, suitcasing him,
keeping him for himself, unwilling to leave him, the corpse
that he is, dead and lonely in the tomb, to remain, his pockets
candied, Cleveland and the gang exhausting a wide range
of resurrecting techniques, inviting local animals to lick at
the seams, for, despite their failure, an inability to achieve
godhood, Cleveland could create something yet, and what
else is godhood but that?

IRREGULAR

LIMBS

1////

They hadn't killed him, they'd found him that way. It was pleasant weather and they were wearing jackets, hands in their pockets, when they noticed a depression in the timothy of Jepson's empty lot. They were on their way to the corner store for sodas when they noticed this depression in the timothy-grass and found Alexander, Gary Shuman's older brother, with his eyes closed lying there in the middle of it. They were three boys in their jackets and the three of them stood over him for a while, over Alexander, before finding a nearby stick to prod him with in the ribs and the face. He ended up being alive, so they resumed walking to the corner store as they'd planned to, before finding Alexander out there in the grass with his eyes closed. Their names were Devin, Gavin, and Curtis.

The town—its roads and buildings and people—was generally asleep, or nearly asleep, and in the fall was even more so. It was early fall, late in the afternoon, and the boys, after purchasing bottles of sarsaparilla and glugging them down, were heading back home when they noticed, for a second time, the grass stamped down in the middle of Jepson's empty lot. They sorted their way again through the high timothy. Jepson's empty lot had once been a drive-in cinema and it still had an enormous screen, which was rotting, and a dilapidated projection house and a gateway marquee that was empty except for three Es. The parking lot had long been overrun by timothy-grass. But out in the middle of the timothy Alexander was lying curled up, fetal, and they noticed that now he was missing most of his left arm. It wasn't like that before. They all agreed that the arm had still been intact when they found him in the field only an hour or less earlier. The boys stood over Alexander with his eyes still closed, as before, but now with his arm sawed off, the hole in his shoulder gaping and pulsing with purplish mess and bone. Before there had been an arm and now there was not an arm anywhere.

They found the stick again and used it and he ended up being alive, so the boys finished what was left of their sarsaparillas before hurling the bottles against the projection house. They wiped their mouths and wondered if Alexander was probably dying and if Gary Shuman would be okay with his older brother dying with his eyes closed in the middle of Bart Jepson's empty lot without one of his arms. It was an open wound but it seemed to be mostly done letting go of the wet purple parts of Alexander. Most of that part of Alexander was in the grass now, purpling the yellow-dry stalks of timothy. It was convenient that Alexander's T-shirt remained pretty clean, and his pants, not much blood on him, so that the boys weren't averse to moving him, because they decided that was what was appropriate, though they hadn't agreed upon where he should be moved to. There were certain aesthetic advantages to Alexander lying alone without his one arm, dying in the timothy-grass, they agreed about this. But they knew that if they were Gary Shuman and their older brother Alexander was left to die out here, that they'd have wished it differently. Anywhere, they figured, would be better, socially, for Alexander to die, other than here.

The three boys—Devin, Gavin, and Curtis—carried Alexander slowly, taking great care to keep him from limply skimming the sidewalks as they lifted, two of them holding a leg each and the other hanging on around the shoulder that still had an arm. Because Alexander was heavy, even for the three of them, they often had to take breaks, laying Alexander down in the lawns of whoever's yard they were passing when he was slipping from their fingers. Eventually though, they hefted him to where they agreed he should be left, placing him gingerly over the ground at the entrance of the town's cemetery.

Giving themselves some distance from Alexander after they'd laid him down, the three boys looked and right away recognized their error. How presumptuous! They were immature, obvious, and stupid. That much they could agree on.

It was a convenient location but leaving him there was tactless.

He was still alive, so again they lifted him up, one limb per boy, and carried him to where it was obvious, they agreed, they should have first thought to leave him dying— though they stopped themselves once to make sure they weren't making another sloppy decision.

Alexander, Gary Shuman's older brother, had been boyfriend-girlfriend with Jessica Upton since before the boys could remember. She lived near the cemetery, which the boys agreed was a coincidence. Their memory of Alexander and Jessica was uncomfortable, since they'd often seen them standing, pressed together outside the corner store where they bought sarsaparillas, hands in each other's pockets. Once, when Curtis was away, Devin and Gavin stumbled into a terrible mess behind the Silkworks Mall, finding Alexander boyfriend-girlfriending with Jessica in a way that seemed unreasonable to be happening back there. Afterwards, when the two told it to Curtis, Curtis was upset that he hadn't been there, but Devin and Gavin promised him that if he had that he'd have wished he hadn't.

Gary Shuman's older brother Alexander was long and androgynous, and they laid him down on his side, his back facing Jessica Upton's front door. They debated ringing the doorbell but decided against it. They left him on the front porch, his pale skin glowing under the porch light.

It was evening, or it was starting to be evening, and the sky was pinking some and there were clouds, so the boys felt they needed to return to their respective homes and eat their respective dinners. They made an agreement, however. They agreed to return afterward, to meet later that evening in front of Jessica's house to ensure that Alexander had been, in some way, attended to. That Gary Shuman wouldn't be disappointed in how Alexander spent his final living hours.

Devin, at home, ate honey-grilled salmon over rice. Gavin ate vegetable hamburgers with crisscross French fries and watched a portion of the 1988 Summer Olympics with his father, who coached the high school track team. Alexander was a long-distance runner and Gavin's father knew him well in that capacity, but Gavin didn't tell him about Alexander's arm or how his eyes were closed. Curtis ate popcorn with his older sister, who was in charge while his parents were out for the night.

Devin, Gavin, and Curtis, and their families, or portions of their families, spent their evenings together the way they were supposed to, being Americans, and active churchgoers, except their fathers.

When the three boys returned to Jessica Upton's front porch, Alexander was gone. They decided that Jessica had found him there and had dragged his body into her bedroom where she held his head to her chest and cried into his hair. They decided that Jessica Upton and Gary Shuman's older brother were in love and that this was as Gary would have wanted it—and Alexander too, if he'd been asked beforehand, when he still had the ability to respond.

They became uncertain, however, because they noticed that the purple part of

Alexander, the open part, hadn't fallen out anywhere or streaked anywhere on the cement, as it might've if he'd been dragged, and they'd've suspected as much, since Jessica wouldn't have been able to lift him herself. It was slightly disconcerting, so they approached the Upton home, ringing the doorbell, and then in haste squirmed nervously on the porch. They were uncertain about confronting Jessica Upton about her dying, armless boyfriend, Alexander, whom they'd left there over an hour or more earlier. How would they say what they wanted? What could they do, so as to inflict the smallest possible injury, while still gathering the information they needed in order to satisfy this responsibility to Gary Shuman that they felt was theirs? When the entryway light lit up, and the door opened, they saw it was Jessica, and they saw her face, and they realized that Alexander was not in the house, that Jessica had not seen him at all, and did not know that he had closed his eyes and that his arm, his left arm, was no longer attached to his shoulder, and they didn't say anything, they simply listened to her say, Hi, and, What's up? And then they turned around, each of them, and walked away.

The boys return to Jepson's empty lot instinctively. The enormous white movie screen emanates something like light in the dark, but otherwise it is simply dark. Dark dark. There is no way to see out in the field whether or not there is something out in the field. They stop under the marquee: EEE. They don't look at each other. There is a campfire smell from somewhere nearby but there isn't any campfire light. They look at each other before sorting their way through the field again, for the third time that day. It is cool, but it is pleasant and their jackets are sufficient as they aim themselves in the general direction of where they first found Gary Shuman's older brother. They circle around a bit in the timothy before Curtis almost falls into a largish hole, longish, and he tells the other two to watch out for it and they do. When they are all around the hole, which, they agree, was not there earlier that day, they try looking for things they might drop into it and find a stone. They drop the stone in and then think that maybe they forgot to listen for it to land and so they search for another stone to drop in but they do not find one. Gavin kicks some dirt into the hole and they listen to the sand shower and spread through the air. Devin looks at Gavin and then over at Curtis. It is dark enough that you couldn't see what a person's expression was if they were a foot away from you. They start talking to each other, agreeing on things. Concrete things and ambiguities. They have a conversation. Gavin does most of the talking, first to Devin and then to both Devin and Curtis. Curtis says something, then Devin. Devin talks to Gavin individually and then to both Gavin and Curtis together. Curtis, this time, does not agree. They are not in agreement. The campfire smell thickens, feels closer, and coming from the largish, longish hole the boys notice a slow, blurred cooing, like language wetted and then handled within the palm of one's hand. It floats up into the space between them, hovering over the hole, but is mostly indistinguishable. Gavin gets down on his hands and knees, leans in over the hole and listens closer. More cooing—slow, blurred—but softer, evaporating. Curtis walks away from the pit a few paces, stands, walks back. They discuss, one last time, Gary Shuman, and imagine him imagining Alexander's last breath and wonder to themselves whether—if Alexander is down there, down against the dirt floor and walls—if that's enough.

They think it's worse than before. That this won't do at all. Curtis is reluctant, to be sure. Gavin and Devin, however, know that there is little if any time for Alexander to be alive if he or anyone is down at the bottom of the largish, longish hole. They grab Curtis by the arms and he is struggling backwards, but they pull him into the hole and he falls to the bottom. He struggles so much that he almost pulls Devin in with him, but he doesn't and only Curtis falls into the hole that hadn't been there before.

Curtis lands on something softish that gives a little bit and it's a body and he is lying on the body wheezing because some of the wind's been knocked out of him the way his gut's fallen into the body at the bottom of the hole. Or rather, it's the stone that's knocked the wind out of him, lying on top of the body. Curtis has fallen flat onto the stone that they'd dropped into the hole onto the body and he's coughing and wheezing and trying to acclimate himself to the darkness, lit only by a rectangle of dark sky and clouds overhead.

Curtis will yell violently at Devin and Gavin before tentatively confirming there's a body down there with him. He will talk about how dark it is and how he feels out of his wits and that the body could be anyone's body. Devin and Gavin will ask whether the body has one arm or two, and Curtis, in a state of panic, will only scream at them, frantically, to be helped out of the hole. When they do not respond, he will stand up, cautiously, his stomach still in knots, and try to grab at the walls of the hole, which will crumble in his fingers.

Devin and Gavin will eventually make it back to Jessica's house. They will have agreed that this is the appropriate thing to do. They will consider that Alexander is likely dead and, for convenience sake, will be left in that hole, buried there, when all's said and done, but that regardless, Gary Shuman would want his brother's girlfriend, Jessica Upton, to hear about it first. They will say they know this is the right thing because they, Devin and Gavin, know the lengths to which Jessica and Alexander have boyfriend-girlfriended behind the Silkworks Mall.

After the time it takes to convince Jessica to leave her home in the late evening with the two younger boys, their jackets no longer sufficient, though their adrenaline evening out their body temperature, the three will return to Bart Jepson's empty lot, wade through the timothy-grass, and Jessica, who will have a flashlight—the boys will recommend it—will find herself at the edge of the hole dug in the middle of the empty lot, flashing the light down in.

Curtis will be down there, his eyes closed, his left arm missing.

2////

Alexander would soon find himself in a position where he would be standing over three boys in his brother's year, each of them with their legs sheared off just above the knees. He would recognize their faces, know that Gary had been in classes with them, had associated with them, and that if they hadn't been friends, they'd at least been acquaintances. They are not boys that he would have taken any thought of before discovering them there, each in a different position: one on his back, one on his stomach, one on his side.

As it was, Alexander sat with his long back arching away from the bench where he was seated, centering his chin over his milkshake. He had long arms and legs, and facial features that were sharp, distinct, as if cut from particular kinds of stone. His girlfriend, Jessica Upton, sat opposite from him, eating finger-thick French fries. They often spent time where they were, sitting in the corner booth of the town's outskirt diner, which took on most of the traffic passing by on the nearby highway. It wasn't all that near to the highway, but the diner had spent advertising money on a series of billboards that acclaimed its one-of-a-kind-ness, a claim that could be disputed, and that's where they were. The general population of the town didn't frequent the diner much and that's why Alexander and Jessica went there. The town was sleepy, or could be called sleepy. Jessica called Alexander Alex.

Jessica told Alex something that made Alex laugh and the two of them grabbed their items—Jessica's fries and Alexander's milkshake—and left the diner. Alexander had a 1987 Toyota Chaser that was white and old-looking and he and Jessica ran out to it. Alexander unlocked the doors and they got in. Alexander started the car and they drove off, away from the diner, and into town.

After they did some boyfriend-girlfriend things that Jessica's parents were worried about and that Alexander's mother was worried about too (but not his father because his father was dead), Alexander dropped Jessica off at her home, a couple or more blocks from the cemetery. Jessica's parents asked where she'd been and she told them that she was with Bella even though she was with Alexander. Her parents had seen Alexander's car though and told Jessica not to lie to them and then Jessica lied and said that Alex was over at Bella's house with her and some other kids were over there too and that Alex just gave her a ride home is all. Her parents looked at her sternly, disbelieving, and told her to stick around because it was almost dinner.

After her parents had returned to the kitchen, her mother cooking and her father talking to her mother about how he knew that Jessica was lying, Jessica walked out the back door of the house, making sure to open and close the door as quietly as possible. Once outside, Jessica escaped onto the adjacent street and walked, like she liked to do, toward the old bridge. The bridge was ten or less blocks from her home and Jessica had spent a lot of time by herself walking to and from the bridge. It was a bridge for trains and was out of use and rusting and grass had found ways to grow even in the middle of the tracks and Jessica liked to go down to the area under the bridge and read or just watch the stream which ran through there and that's where she went when she wanted to be by herself. Even Alex didn't know about it. Before arriving where she was going, Jessica passed the large open fields of timothy-grass that grew on the undeveloped side—the bridge-side—of the street she walked. She noticed something shadowy, deep in the grass, and thought there might be a bison felled out there, because she had seen bison before that had escaped from the ranch north of their town and had been shot. She was enamored by bison in a way she couldn't describe and wanted to see one up close, and it was getting darker, so she walked out toward the shadowy area, closer because she couldn't see very well, and realized, as she approached, that she should be able to see it by now, if it were a bison. And then, out there—in the shadowy patch of timothy—she found three boys lying on the ground, unmoving, with their eyes closed. She knelt down and touched their faces with her hands. She touched their chests. They were still alive, so she left, went down to down-under-the-bridge, spent time there for a little bit and then went for Alex.

Jessica, when she got there, said something to Alexander's mother that made Alexander's mother uneasy, but Alexander's mother retrieved Alexander just the same. Jessica could see Gary in at the kitchen table reading a magazine and Gary looked up and looked at Jessica as Jessica and Alexander were leaving.

In the car, Alex kisses Jessica playfully on the mouth and Jessica kisses back and they do this for a minute before Jessica tells Alex she wants him to see something and they drive there.

It's pretty late now. Alexander doesn't care sometimes about driving into the timothy-grass with his 1987 Toyota Chaser. It's dark so he says he wants to get the headlights on the spot where they want to go. The timothy folds under the car and Alexander drives right up to the spot, opens the door—Jessica too—and they sort through it to the boys, who are still there, lying in a nest of timothy. Alexander asks Jessica about the legs and she says that before there were legs. The legs aren't all-the-way gone, though, only half-gone. It's getting colder so Jessica sits on the hood of the car, still warm from the heat of the engine, and Alexander hugs his arms around his body. He stands, watching the boys, thinking they're dead. He flips the one on his stomach over onto his back and sees that they all have their eyes closed.

Alexander stands for a long time looking at the parts of their missing legs, at the innards of their thighs, and find himself confused that—though hacked through, revealing muscle and bone—there is little if any mess pooling in the grass beneath their stumps. They must have been transported here, he thinks, from wherever it was that they had been reduced to having nothing from the knees down. The grass is clean.

It's a long time before they figure out that they're still alive.

Jessica asks Alexander to sit next to her and he does, keeping an eye on the boys. Jessica nuzzles into Alexander's neck area to kiss at him while he watches the boys. After she quits, she says she's cold and gets back in the car. Alexander backs out of the timothy and drives her home but drops her off at the cemetery so that her parents don't see it's him dropping her off.

Alexander drives back past the open field where he'd just been with Jessica, and sees that there is something large, like a bear, out in the area where he had just seen three boys without legs, boys with their eyes closed, lying. He slows but keeps driving. His window's down and he hears something like a throaty bark in the air. A couple more blocks and he stops the car. He shifts it into reverse for a second and waits, and then puts it back into drive.

In the morning, Alexander will get up early and wake his brother, Gary, telling him he wants to show him something. In the mornings, the town is white with sun as if it will never become dark again. The town seems to yawn in the mornings. They will drive out by the small river, something like a stream, and over into the field near where the old train bridge is. Their windows will be down and it will smell like there's been a fire nearby. Alexander will try to intuit the area where the boys were but will fail and keep driving through the timothy-grass, circling, and Gary, his brother, will be quiet and confused. The fire smell, like a campfire, will become too strong and the boys will roll up their windows. It will become obvious to Alexander that the three boys are gone. Gary will ask what it is that Alexander wants to show him. Alexander will say it's nothing and tell Gary to get out of the car in the middle of the field, and Alexander, not out of any disdain for his brother, or embarrassment, but out of confusion, and an odd sense of urgency, will leave Gary there. Gary will just be standing there. Alexander will say, I'll be right back, and will drive back through the field and onto the road and then off, out of sight, towards the cemetery.

He will not understand why Jessica will be sitting on her front porch, waiting for him, with a bucket of black paint.

3////

The town is predictably sleepy by nature of its size and location. It sits isolated, far enough away from other towns to warrant something approaching loneliness in the eaves of its architecture and the attitude of its homes. People, when they speak of the town, when they pass through it in their cars and trucks, mention how tired the town seems, how quiet. It is not unlike other similarly isolated towns, towns wherein the houses have situated themselves modestly atop flat expanses of unobstructed land. It is just like those kinds of towns. In many ways it's the same town. In every way, perhaps, it is exactly that town, repeated.

The town, whatever number of towns it actually is, however ubiquitous, is what it is by being itself, alone, individual, and nearly asleep. Its sleepiness is partially an accident. Something about the uniformity of the town's construction—the meticulous gridding of the streets and the economy with which the town has maintained itself for so long, its sleepy steadfastness—has lulled the population of the town into an unintended hibernation. Without any fuss or discussion, the townspeople, each involved in the particularities of who they are in the town—police officer, schoolteacher, baker, etc.—leave their places of business and return to their homes. There they eat meals with their families, remove their shoes, and lie down in their beds. They close their eyes and, shortly, all of them are asleep, inaudibly humming the songs of sleeping, breathing.

It stays this way for weeks. Or just over a week. The townspeople lying in their beds, not comatose, for there are occasional shufflings under the sheets and some sleeptalking, but it is almost, or nearly, a coma that they're in. And it isn't only the people but the buildings, the walls, and the circuitry running within the walls, in addition to the appliances and the furniture—everything, except possibly the small river running along the southern end of the town, is slumbering. It's literally a sleeping town, before, well, something else.

Something, similar to a woman in a dress, but much larger than a woman, is awake and building a pyre in the field behind the high school. Something similar to a woman in appearance, but proportionally more like a bear, or like something even slightly larger than a bear. Women stop growing and eventually die and some even grow smaller but they do not become this large. It is dirty and its movements do not resemble the women of the town, but it appears to be a very tall woman, wearing a dress. In the distance the sun is in the process of setting on the town, as has become its habit.

So, it gets darker.

The blaze from the pyre casts an orange glow against the walls of the school and those of the nearby houses, and the windows of the houses shine with the reflection of the great flames. The inhumanly tall woman walks through the town, dark with sleep, and heavy with the smell of campfire smoke from the pyre. She is carrying a heavy bucket filled with black paint, or oil, and in her opposite hand she carries a wide paintbrush.

Sidling up to one of the town's houses, the woman crouches down, staring into the unlit interior. She is close enough to the pyre that it sets her aglow, if only faintly, her massive figure low-humming a blackish orange. Pressing her face against the skin of the house, as if listening, she drags her face along its siding. She finds the front door and opens it. The dimensions of the home demand that the tall woman stoop down and struggle sideways to enter. Upon entering the home, the tall woman says something, a word, or something the size and shape of a word while being something else altogether. As darkness has overcome the town, she turns on a light in the house. She lumbers up the stairs with her bucket and paintbrush, down the hallway, turning the lights on as she crouches her way through the space. Everywhere within the house requires her to hunker down, always with some part of her in contact with either a wall or the ceiling, the home is so small. She reaches the hallway's end and enters into a room, finds a boy sleeping. She turns on the light, heedless, and approaches the bed. The boy remains asleep. He is tall for a boy, almost an adult, and with a thin athletic build. There is something androgynous in his sinuous composition. The tall, dirty woman looms over him, obstructing the ceiling lamp, shadowing him. She says something hushed, like a word, over the boy. Then she pulls the boy's sheets from his body. He is wearing a white T-shirt and grey sweatpants. The woman proceeds to dip the paintbrush into the paint, or oil, and paints the boy's left arm black, lifting it in order to coat it on all sides, leaving the scene messy and black before parting. Her footsteps and the way her body scrapes against the walls of the home amplify against the town's sleepy quietness.

The tall woman, or creature, continues in this fashion— entering and departing from homes, leaving a trail of opened front doors and lights left on, and townspeople, asleep in their beds, some fraction of them with body parts painted black, or portions of body parts, their arms or legs—before entering a home set near the cemetery. The tall woman enters through the doorway, grunting and turning on the lights—the town sleeping sleeping sleeping—and, finding her way through the cramped hallway, finally enters into the room where one sits awake. A young woman, only a girl. The tall woman, reaching in through the doorway and turning on the light, sees the girl, sitting, staring. She is silent. The tall woman pauses, stares back at the girl through heavy strands of dirtied hair, then pulls herself into the room. Setting her black bucket next to the bed, the tall creature patiently presses the girl down onto her pillow, whispers an inhuman whisper, then pulls her filthy black brush through the girl's hair and across her face. The girl is too paralyzed to speak.

The tall woman grabs the girl by the hair, the girl choking on paint, and pulls her from her bed and down into the hallway. She leaves her paint and brush on the girl's bedroom carpet. She pulls the girl and the girl struggles, her eyes closed in oil, or oil-black paint. The creature, massive and grimy, drags the girl across lawns and sidewalks and the gravel of the roads, in the middle-night dark, and the girl ceases struggling, and, her eyes blacked with paint, her eyes cease blinking and finally close.

Once back at the pyre, the tall woman releases the girl onto the field of grass. The pyre is nearly burned through and the sun is preparing to rise. The town, for all its geometry, its neatly organized sidewalks and its outskirts, fields of yellowed timothy-grass and scattered gatherings of trees, can no longer sustain its sleeping. Its buildings roll their shoulders, their wooden joints creaking within them. Microwaves restore their settings, their digital clocks blinking to be reset. Refrigerators reinstate their droning motors, buzzing in the morning light. The townspeople open their eyes and it's a slow-waking moment, a moment of calm confusion—I left the lights on? Where are my shoes? Alex, what's that on your arm? It's not until the future that anyone realizes anything about how long the town's been sleeping. Animals begin to approach the town again, birds and small mammals. The school's principal is punctual and pulls into the parking lot, smells the heavy smokiness of the burnt pyre, and walks out into the field behind the school. In addition to the crumbling black ashes of the pyre, there is a deep hole in the middle of the field. He approaches the hole and looks down into it. It is a dark hole and he spends a fair amount of time looking, his eyes adjusting to the dimness. Once he feels he understands what it is, he frowns. He enters the school using his key and tidies up some things in his office and then makes a phone call.

The town remains drowsy, but bright. It's a small town and there is an energy unique to the town, as in other towns that are exactly the same as the town. It is an energy bred of the town's particular construction, its layout, which breeds a genial nature among its citizens.

Before long, a handful—then a crowd—of people are gathered around the hole. A fraction or more of the crowd have parts of themselves painted black, some with their legs from their knees down, some their arms, others portions of their hips, torsos, and thighs. They are all confused, and some of them are worried about the paint, however, this becomes unimportant once they've looked down into the hole. Every individual who looks down into the hole frowns in disappointment. There are differing opinions about what it is exactly they are looking at, but most agree it is something disappointing and many begin to pray. Before long it is noted that if it is what some think it is, the majority of them, then the boyfriend must be contacted. The boyfriend's brother is present and sprints home to fetch him.

When the boyfriend finally arrives, he is tall and athletic

and hesitates to approach. His left arm is painted black. As he approaches, the crowd opens, creating a path. He reaches the edge of the hole and looks down. Within the crowd, someone yells something. Then someone else. They want to know if it is what they think it is. They want a positive identification. The boyfriend stands over the hole for a long time, staring down into the darkness. Everyone remains quiet, and they're there long enough that some among the townspeople leave. There is still a sizable crowd, however, when the boyfriend blinks twice, coughs, and leaves. A handful of the town trail behind him, out of curiosity. Some in the crowd yell out after him, demanding to know what he saw. The crowd weakens, its individual parts separating and expanding into the field and back into the town. A police officer arrives and begins to break things up. The walls and windows of the homes and buildings look on, anxious, nervous that, come nightfall, they won't be able to sleep.

THE GARY CHAOS

A mistake can be made about Gary that he's alive. The way his arms move, his legs. He has, however, as of late, been spending his time posthumously—not all living. He'll die eventually. Maybe someday his guts will hemorrhage somehow—he's driving, gliding off into a slope of grass, grabbing at his stomach, who knows? No one knows. But whether or not in the future he's half-buried in his car— insides filling, hood on fire, whatnot—here he is, now, dead and doubled.

Doubled because he's being followed. Yes, by this point Gary has Gary behind him with his dog and they're following him. Garys. It's been years now, this happening— him following him, Gary after Gary—because, of course, Gary'd been married for a while, and though he didn't have any children, he did have, or his wife had had, when they were still married, a child. Peradventure some creativity. And—no surprise—the baby's born stillborn, after his father.

That's not all the way true: Gary, with his wife, earlier conceived a living son, Alex. Alex, though, one of his arms fell off. Maybe drugs. Don't worry about Alex. Gary spending his time posthumously doesn't mean he's depressed when Alex loses his arm. Though, yes, they were depressed. Alex disappeared into armlessness. Everyone was depressed. That's not important. Doubling is important. Doubling is saying, afterward—after Alex—Gary becomes Garys. Two.

And, as planned, Gary and his wife divorce. The hospital recommends burying the baby. Others too. At the funeral, Gary's ex-wife's sister sings a ballad over the casket. *Sing the requiem too*, Gary says, and Gary's ex-wife's sister's husband puts his hand on Gary's shoulder. *Let it go*, he's saying, his hand. And they eat all the food, everyone, though not Gary. Gary doesn't eat food posthumously. At some point, little dead baby Gary gets out of his casket when everyone's eating food and no one knows where he is and fifteen, maybe twenty, years later, Gary has Gary behind him with his dog and they're following him.

Gary doesn't care one way or the other, and neither does Gary, about following and being followed, but Gary himself opts into a northeastern writer's colony and the colony says Gary and his dog need to give Gary both time and space. They hand him a brochure and that's what it says: *both time and space*. So no more following, it appears. Because of a writer's colony. Because Gary's always considered the possibility.

Gary and his dog will die eventually. Gary in particular (Gary's son.) Maybe Gary's dog will eat parts of Gary when Gary dies, like some dogs have been reported to do, but dead Gary isn't being eaten by his dog yet. Eventually, though, maybe his stomach's hemorrhaging somehow and he rolls down the stairs, and at the bottom, after some days, there's the dog.

Northeast, people love Gary's writing because he's doing it posthumously and that revs everyone up about being dead and having shoeboxes with unpublished manuscripts buried in their backyards. Everyone at the colony is passing around their depression medications and writing, and everyone is giving Gary space and talking about Gary. The director of the writer's colony, a woman, asks Gary if he's inclined to make a relationship out of their proximity. *Oh*, Gary thinks, *necrophilia or whatever*, and he writes a novel.

Gary's novel is accepted for publication posthumously. Gary uses his advance to live in the basement of an apartment building. It's adequately coffin-like and Gary finds he prefers subterranean living. The book people who are publishing Gary's book call him. They're disappointed to hear Gary is still moving around, giving the appearance of living, and feel this is a breach of contract. They're holding off publishing, they tell Gary, until Gary's all the way dead and not moving. Gary smokes hundreds of cigarettes and falls asleep.

Gary's ex-wife's Maggie's name is Maggie. In the aftermath of Garys' posthumously following and being followed, respectively, Maggie turns the corner, metaphorically speaking. Though literally, at the mall, she also turns the corner, into a newer Gary, by coincidence. It's there, in the small town mall, shoppers drifting sleepily from store to store, that Maggie finds her hand handling a new Gary and they're there excusing themselves, shyly, for becoming entangled. Gary has a nametag for policing the mall. *Apparently I'm weak for Garys*, says Maggie. New Gary, via his hip-harnessed walkie-talkie, receives this feed: *Armless juvenile back-seating in the northern parking lot.*

New Gary visits Maggie after work and finds Gary, Maggie's stillborn son, with his dog in the front yard. New Gary introduces himself to Gary, though before Gary has a chance to respond, Maggie's opened the front door and beckons Gary to please come in, don't worry about Gary. New Gary eyes the boy, the dog, as he walks towards Maggie, the dog pulling at the boy's shirtsleeve like a rag toy. Maggie explains she doesn't know why but that seems to be her son Gary who was stillborn and went missing twenty years ago, but there he is in the front yard, for some reason.

Gary, when he's evicted from his basement apartment, returns to his sleepy hometown because he isn't quite all the way dead yet and wants to be closer by for when he needs to be buried, which is on the horizon, he feels. Inexplicably, he finds himself behind Gary, his stillborn son, and Gary's dog, and he's following them. Gary follows Gary as he walks the neighborhood sidewalks in a centripetal manner, finally arriving at the home of his ex-wife, Maggie. Maggie lives where Maggie and Gary used to live together, though never their stillborn son Gary, who was presumed dead, and was, but reemerged from absenteeism when he began following Gary and no one knew how he'd gathered a pet dog in the process. All this being well after the divorce.

Maggie's surprised to see Gary hasn't died all the way yet and Gary's surprised that Maggie's moved on and seems to be having sex with Gary again, but not Gary Gary, a new Gary—*He's* New *Gary*, Maggie says—and stillborn Gary makes his way into the house because Maggie and New Gary've left the front door open and someone calls the police. The Garys, though, seem to be getting along, Gary being apathetic in his posthumous affect, and Gary, too, sitting on the couch, the dog on the rug, though New Gary, despite being cordial, is a bit messed up, Maggie can tell, his face twisting in the presence of so much dead Gary baggage.

When the police arrive, Maggie is berating Gary for operating posthumously, for having the gall to not be all the way dead yet, and what right does he have to get to die twice? Gary looks pathetically at the ground as New Gary speaks to the deputy. The deputy, an older-looking young woman, asks New Gary to leave her alone, she's not some mall cop, she's for real, and to get out of the way, I need to taze this shithead.

Tazing Gary is anti-climactic and Maggie's dissatisfied, as is the deputy police officer, and the two women leave the scene of Gary posthumously lying on the front lawn, Maggie into her home, the police officer into her patrol vehicle, and there New Gary is, left alone with Gary, who is experiencing, he expects, his second death (at least he hopes). New Gary looks at Gary and apologizes, before filling his mouth with dirt from the nearby garden.

Maggie is holding Gary, her son, on the couch, when she hears Gary bare-knuckling against the front door and the dog barking. *That's him, that's New Gary.* Gary out front on the front lawn has his mouth filled with dirt and he's looking into the sky. Stillborn Gary gets the feeling there's no death for the already dead, though he's unwilling to say so. New Gary, knocking and calmly calling for Maggie, stating his profession and how they met at the mall earlier that day, and he was indeed a certified safety officer, considers, however briefly, what it means to live not living and if it is a preferable solution to uncertainty and the disappointment of almost-happiness. Maggie, when the knocking won't stop and her son's as dead as he's ever been, she too thinks, who doesn't want a death of some kind in this life, who wouldn't love living posthumously? Gets-angry-Gary was a name ever-named in her presence, remembering Alex, her Alex—sweet Alex—who lost his arm and couldn't find it anywhere, and regardless, kept living until he was dead or missing—certainly missing—but never willing to live in-between life and death in her presence. And when she's thinking all this, she's ascended the stairs and entered her bedroom and is lying on her bed, midafternoon, preparing to go to sleep—Garyless, if possible.

CONRAD DILLINGER'S

INEVITABLE DEATH

Someday.

247

ACKNOWLEDGMENTS

Many thanks to the following journals in which these stories first appeared:

"The Wreath Option" & "Sven Rearranged," *Caketrain*
"Temporary Goliath Temporarily," *Black Warrior Review*
"New Animals," *The Chattahoochee Review*
"Herbert 2b Makes a Mess of the Locals" & "Well-wishing the Weight of Something Kevinly Piecemeal," *Sleepingfish*
"Josh Henderson Is Anne Boleyn," *Fairy Tale Review*
"Winifred, Not a Horse," *Bat City Review*
"Submerge/Ascend," *Pear Noir!*
"Arto's Headspace," *Fourteen Hills*
"Paul's Tomb: A Triumph," *The Collagist*
"Irregular Limbs," *Ninth Letter*
"The Gary Chaos," *The Rupture*
"Conrad Dillinger's Inevitable Death," *The Rumpus*

Special thanks also to Derek White, Brian Evenson, Thalia Field, Vi Khi Nao, Carole Maso, Renee Gladman, Mona Awad, John Madera, S. Tourjee, Evelyn Hampton, and Angela Ferraiolo. Additionally, many thanks to Karen Brennan, Elisa Glick, Natanya Ann Pulley, Trudy Lewis, Tanya McQueen, Angie Metro, Nathan Hauke, and Chris Dunsmore. Thanks to Sam Cheney. And most importantly, thanks to Erin.

ABOUT THE AUTHOR

Nick Francis Potter is a writer, multi-media artist, educator, and the Director of Undergraduate Studies for the School of Visual Studies at the University of Missouri. In addition to *New Animals*, winner of the Subito Press Prize for Innovative Prose, he is the author of *Big Gorgeous Jazz Machine* (Driftwood Press) and *Static Gifs* (Greying Ghost). He has exhibited paintings and installations in various galleries nationally, often in collaboration with wife and partner, Erin. He lives in Columbia, MO with his wife, dog, and two children.